PHILLIP DAVIS

Jack-o'-Lightning

First published by Pepperming Lightning Press 2020

Copyright © 2020 by Phillip Davis

First edition

ISBN: 9780692706190

This book was professionally typeset on Reedsy.
Find out more at reedsy.com

For anyone who has overcome fear

Contents

Acknowledgement   iv

Prologue   v

I   Part One

Chapter 1   3

Chapter 2   7

Chapter 3   14

Chapter 4   19

Chapter 5   26

Chapter 6   29

Chapter 7   32

Chapter 8   38

Chapter 9   46

Chapter 10   54

II   Part Two

Chapter 11   63

Chapter 12   67

Chapter 13   71

Chapter 14   75

Chapter 15   78

Chapter 16   82

Chapter 17   88

Chapter 18   96

Chapter 19   102

Chapter 20   108

Chapter 21   114

Chapter 22   117

III   Part Three

Chapter 23   125

Chapter 24   129

Chapter 25   132

Chapter 26   137

Chapter 27   142

Chapter 28   149

Chapter 29   153

Chapter 30   159

Chapter 31   165

Chapter 32   170

Chapter 33   173

Chapter 34   178

Chapter 35   183

Chapter 36   186

Chapter 37   188

Chapter 38   193

Epilogue   197
About the Author   198
Also by Phillip Davis   199

Acknowledgement

The idea for this novel was born in text-message conversations with my dear friend Corey Rose. Like many of our conversations, it took turns into places I hadn't expected. Were it not for Mr. Rose, many of my projects would never get off the ground.

I owe my wife for her patience and support. Without her, I'd never have overcome the fear of putting pen to paper nor of releasing what I've written into the world.

I also owe a great thanks to "Lia the Editor" for her contributions above and beyond the call of duty and to Mostafa Kamal for his feedback as the novel's first reader.

I would also like to thank the faithful friends of the Peppermint Lightning family. You know who you are. -PD

Prologue

Once, there were many worlds, not just *this* one and the *other one*. For lifetimes, the ways between these worlds were many and easily crossed. Humanity wandered into the realm of the gods, fairies, places of wonder and terror that would come to be known by names like heaven and hell, Bhuva Loka, and Valhalla. Man spent little time defining the borders, but as the strength of this world grew, as man evolved and increased their ambition, the separation between worlds grew more distinct.

The magic of Fae, for example, lost its importance in the lives and eventually the stories of mankind. Finding ways in and out became more difficult, and these worlds became set apart from one another. With the world of man increasingly cut off, the denizens of these other worlds turned their focus to one another. Those in the realms of the dead, of spirits, of the arcane easily passed from one to the other. It was only the realm of man that remained separate.

Over time, a barrier developed. Man taught itself to fear the other worlds, the unknown, the places of dreams and nightmares. Fear built a wall. Fear made passage from one place to another nearly impossible. The dead could still pass to the underworld, one of the many places beyond the veil, but the dead could not travel back with the ease that had been for so long the way of things.

A guardian of this veil came into being, though even in my watching it is hard to say when or from where, but a guardian existed nonetheless, and kept the order; enforced what belonged on one side and what belonged on the other.

The worlds on the other side of this veil rose and fell in strength and influence. Their borders grew and shrank and grew again, and by the current age of man, the lines between these worlds were so blurred they were difficult to distinguish. There was little distinction between the paradise lands and those of the lost, or those of the once-omnipotent gods.

A melding of places such as these, a lack of order and structure, made it possible for the ambitious to seize power, to influence, to direct. Some leaders of these lands, powers in these worlds, were peacekeepers and champions for their realms, working to restore what had once defined their homes, their domains. Others were imperialists and sought to annex weaker worlds and gather strength for their own.

Fear and aversion to the misunderstood lent strength to some worlds, worlds where these energies were power and sustenance. And it was in one of these worlds that a vengeful and hungry soul rose to power. One world was not enough for him, but it wasn't the land of Fae or the mountains of Olympus that interested him. It was the realm of man, the world beyond the veil, the strongest of all the worlds, he set his eyes upon. It had once been his home, and he was of a mind that it should be his home again. The world of mankind should become part of the melding worlds he traveled beyond the veil.

* * *

"It's been 200 years!"

"It doesn't matter how long it's been, spirit. You know your passage is forbidden."

"Of course I know that! But I could. I mean—I'm able." Jack had crossed over many times during his 200 years in the underworld. He wasn't supposed to, but he did.

"I don't think pointing out previous violations is the way to convince someone to let you break the rules again, do you?"

"I just need a wee minute. I need to get out of this place and breathe untainted air, visit my kin, go to a pub—"

"You haven't got any kin, and what good is a pub going to do a spirit?"

"A pub is great for the spirits. And I do have kin! I 'ave a lot of kin."

"You had no children."

"My brothers did, lots of them."

"You didn't know any of them and they're long since dead, anyway."

"Their descendants aren't." It was taking effort for Jack not to sound desperate. Desperation would draw suspicion and alert the Keeper of the Gates he was up to something.

"Were I inclined to help you, Jack, this is not a good time."

"And why isn't it a good time? Halloween is always a good time."

"It is not All Hallow's Eve just yet, spirit. And you know why it isn't a good time."

He certainly did, and it was exactly why he wanted to visit the mortal world. He wanted nothing to do with what was happening on this side of the veil.

There was a great wailing in the near distance, a suffering, howling sort of sound. It was a sound common to that realm, but this was loud and sudden and it rose above the usual lamentations. What Jack knew that the Keeper did not was that a group of spirits had just tried to rush the veil and been struck by a blast of pure pain that exploded from the nearly invisible wall.

They were young souls and vulnerable to suggestion, which was precisely why Jack had chosen them. He told them since they had not long lived in the underworld, and their company numbered more than a dozen, they could overwhelm the barrier and crash through. They wanted desperately to return to familiar places before everything changed in the coming storm, and Jack had offered to distract the Keeper long enough for them to get through.

Jack knew they wouldn't make it. He couldn't have cared if they had. They were the distraction. The Keeper's attention was divided for a moment, and a moment was all it took for Jack to disappear from one side of the veil and appear on the other.

* * *

You can't be in the global spotlight and expect privacy. Sidney knew that. She'd done enough TV, magazine, and podcast interviews to know she'd carry the burden of fame for years to come. As the unofficial poster-child for

Christmas spirit, her inbox and social media profiles always got busy shortly before Thanksgiving. Requests for interviews and public appearances at tree lighting ceremonies and pageants flooded in. And she loved it.

She couldn't attend every event she was invited to. She was a junior in high school and had her own life, her own family to attend to, but she never hid from the public. She'd started something and she would not walk away from it. She also couldn't answer every card, tweet, message, or post that came her way. November and December got to be a little overwhelming.

This was October, though. It wasn't out of the ordinary for her to start getting requests for interviews and dates booked, but it was a little early to be getting instant messages from strangers. She'd set up an auto-reply to thank people for reaching out to her and remind them to keep spreading the spark throughout the year. She responded to as many personally as she could, skimming through the messages and picking out the ones that caught her eye. This one caught her eye.

Sidney, you don't know me, but I need your help. I can't think of anyone else who might know what to do. Something is wrong. I know you're very busy, but if you have a few minutes, I think I need to talk to you.

A request for help wasn't uncommon, though they'd become less frequent as Peppermint Lightning continued to grow and spread. People needed advice on how to recharge their community or an individual family member or friend. Someone needed cheering up so they could continue spreading the spark again themselves. This message didn't seem like it was any of those things. It didn't feel the same. It was more desperate somehow.

The message was from someone named Martin Kelly. His profile picture was a jack-o'-lantern. Sidney could see from his profile he was in Massachusetts and was a fan of video games and Avengers movies. Aside from that, all of his information was private.

Sidney responded.

I'm happy to try to help. Can you tell me what the problem is?

The reply was nearly immediate.

Ghosts.

Sidney scratched her head. This was not her area of expertise. Sure, she knew elves pretty well and probably more than most about reindeer, but ghosts, not so much.

I'm sorry. I don't know much about ghosts.

Another quick response

That's okay. He said you don't need to. You know about Peppermint Lightning, and that's sort of related to what's happening here.

Sidney wanted to ask how the two things connected but found she was more intrigued by the idea a ghost had told Martin to contact her. Before the events of the Christmas that changed her life, she might have thought the kid was just crazy, but she'd learned a thing or two about what seems crazy since then. She typed another message.

The ghost told you to contact me?

Yes. Kind of.

So, you talk to this ghost?

Yes. Well . . . he sort of talks to me but doesn't really listen to what I say.

Any idea why he thinks Peppermint Lightning and ghosts are related?

He didn't really explain that. He just said you could help us. Maybe.

So, what do you need help doing, exactly?

Something bad is coming. A disaster of some kind, I think.

Okay. That doesn't sound good. I'll make a call and see if I can find some kind of connection between PL and ghosts. I'll message you back soon. Are you okay? You aren't in danger, are you?

No. I don't think so. Not yet, anyway. Thank you.

Sidney closed the chat window and opened a new tab on her internet browser. She clicked "North Pole" in her favorites and then the contact link. It was meant to look like a letters-to-Santa form, but she knew her message would go straight to the right hands. She typed, "Emmett, call me when you have a minute. I have a strange question," into the text box and hit send.

* * *

"It's good to hear your voice, Sidney. How are things in Ohio?"

"Fine. Busy with school and the calendar is already starting to fill up. Are you planning on visiting this year?"

"Of course!" Emmett said with cheer. "What is it you needed to talk about? Is everything okay?"

"Yes. Well, with me anyway. I got a strange message though."

"A message?"

"Yeah. Someone sent me a Facebook message. He said he needed help with ghosts."

"Ghosts?"

"Apparently."

"Why did he message you about ghosts? I mean no offense, of course, but I don't think that's what you're known for."

"It sure isn't. He seemed to think, because I know about magic and elves, and Peppermint Lightning, and so on . . ."

"There's something you aren't telling me."

"Apparently, a ghost told him to reach out to me."

"Oh. Well . . . I uh . . ."

"So, I thought I'd reach out to *you* and see what you know about ghosts."

"Nothing really. There aren't any at the North Pole I'm aware of. We all know A Christmas Carol and Mr. Dickens's ghosts, but not much more than that. I can ask around."

"Are they real? Do you know that much? Or is this kid pulling my leg? Maybe he's nuts."

"Oh, no. They are definitely real."

"Know any experts?"

"Not off the top of my head. I'll see what I can find out."

"Great. Thanks, Emmett."

"Anything for you, Sidney. You know that. Talk soon."

"I hope so. Later."

I

Part One

Chapter 1

It was a dark and stormy night. Actually, it wasn't but Martin wished that it was. It was two weeks into autumn, and it had been over 80 degrees all afternoon. The nights were getting a little cooler, but it was a long way from crisp. That hadn't stopped him from convincing his mom it was time to put the hay bales and corn stalks on the front porch.

"Not Halloween yet though, Martin," his mother said.

"I know. It's too early. It *is* October in a few days though, Mom."

"And in October you can turn those pumpkins around."

The prior year, Martin had taken the liberty of carving faces into the thick plastic pumpkins they decorated the porch with every year. He'd put LED lights in them and set them aglow the day the first leaf fell from the maple at the corner of their driveway. His mother had not been thrilled. She was the kind of person who only celebrated holidays for a couple weeks and couldn't endorse a premature decoration. So, Martin had to hide the jack-o'-lantern side until it was time.

Martin had been sitting on the front porch as the sun went down, scribbling away at his math homework when someone spoke to him.

"Boy!" the voice said.

Martin looked around with a start. He peered toward the end of the driveway and up and down the two-foot stone wall that served as a fence along the front yard. He looked over his shoulder through the screen door. Nothing in the front hallway. He picked up his math homework and began to rise.

"Boy! Sit. I need your help."

Martin sat back down. "Who's there?" he asked, a tremble in his voice.

A light flickered to his left. "Here," the voice said.

Martin turned to face the flickering light. A small flame danced inside the plastic pumpkin, but it didn't burn. It was sitting atop the plastic LED bulb. It flared a little when Martin stared into it.

"That's right, m'boy. Right here."

Martin went to stand again, but his legs were jelly and he couldn't make them straighten.

"Please. Sit. Don't shout. Just listen."

Martin furrowed his brow and wondered if maybe the equations he'd been working on had addled his brain. "Who are you?" he managed to ask.

"Most call me Stingy Jack. You . . . you might call me . . . Suffice it to say I know ye. Yer kin, lad."

"So . . . are you a ghost?"

"I am."

"You're the ghost of Stingy Jack? And you're . . . in my pumpkin?"

"Well, not exactly, no. It's a good place for me to come and visit ye, though. It seemed appropriate for context and all."

"Right. Jack of the Lantern."

"So, ya know me then?"

"I guess. I mean, I've heard the story."

"Aye. I'll bet ye have. Don't believe every bit of it, though."

"You said kin?"

"I haven't got the time to do the particulars right now; not strong enough. I need your help."

"Yeah. You said that. What do you mean?"

"There's a storm brewing, lad. They're going to try to come across."

"What storm? Who? Come across what?"

"I haven't got time, lad. You're going to need help. You're going to need to find someone who knows about the powers of this world, of both worlds perhaps. You need to find a way to balance it, boyo."

"Balance what?"

"Martin, please, you've got to help make it right. Please, will you help?"

"I . . . I don't know what—" but he didn't get a chance to finish. The flame

4

vanished and the plastic bulb remained, unmarked, inside a plastic pumpkin with a face carved in.

* * *

He wasn't a truck driver. That had been clear in the first few months of driving a rig up and down the east coast. He wasn't retail material. His customers, and eventually his supervisor, made that clear. He was not an adjunct professor. A few semesters at a community college had taught him that.

Over the years, Dale had learned there were a lot of things he was not. Chief among these was a writer. It wasn't that he didn't write. He wrote prolifically for years, even if no project was ever truly finished. His books languished in neglected spiral notebooks and composition books in milk crates in the attic. He had written a serial short story for Horrorpocolypse magazine when he was a much younger man, but it wasn't a big enough hit for the magazine to call on him to write more. The amount he'd written dwindled as his beard grew longer and more full of silver strands until eventually he stopped entirely.

He wanted to write. A part of him needed to, but he couldn't allow himself the luxury. He wasn't a writer. There were no books with his name on them on the shelf. There were no reviews of his work on publishing websites. Without those things, he simply was not a writer and so didn't allow himself to write.

Except he *did* write. For the past several years Dale had allowed himself one hour of writing a year. In late October or early November there was an hour he set aside when all distractions were eliminated, when all worldly concerns were ignored. On the final night of daylight savings time, when time turned back one hour, Dale allowed himself to write. It was a phantom hour, an extra hour in the year. It didn't really exist for most people. They slept through it. Dale convinced himself that if he wrote during the one extra hour a year people in the United States and Europe were granted, he was getting away with a secret.

Because it was the one time he allowed himself to write, it was particularly special and because it was particularly special, he worked on the same project every year. It was his opus, his masterwork. It was an idea he'd chewed on for years, but since he wasn't a writer, he never put pen to paper until he'd figured out that he had a secret hour he could use.

And when he sat that one hour a year, the words flowed like blood from a fresh wound. That's the kind of simile Dale would use as a horror writer. Images filled his mind's eye. He could hear the voices and the screams of his characters and the literal and figurative demons that plagued them. He could smell the trees, the rain, the wet earth, the city streets where the action took place and feel the pain and joy his characters felt. He was transported. And at the end of the hour, he closed the pages and set the notebook in a drawer to keep it safe until next year.

Chapter 2

"Here's what I can tell you—" Chester told Sidney. "There isn't a lot in the archives specifically about ghosts. The big man doesn't see them as part of our sphere. There is some information about . . . about the other side, though."

"The other side?"

"Yes. It's a little light on details, but from what I can tell there is another place . . . another side of . . . the world, of reality, I suppose. Ghosts seem to come from this place. Or maybe they go to this place. Like I said, the details aren't clear."

"Are we talking about an afterlife?"

"Yes. I think we are, but there seems to be more to it than that."

"Like what?"

"Like things other than just the deceased."

Sidney started to wonder if her old friend was purposely being dodgy about what he knew or if he really didn't know much and was uncomfortable not being able to tell her more. There was definitely a quiver in the little cookie's voice, though.

She said, "Well, is there anything you can tell me that I can use to help Martin?"

"That really boils down to what kind of help he needs."

"And I'm not entirely sure yet myself," Sidney said.

"Right. Well, I don't have a lot to go on. I do think . . . I do think there's someone who can help, though." Sidney could hear Chester's deep breath over the phone, "You see, just like there is Peppermint Lightning, there are other forces in the world, forces that shape and change the way we experience reality."

"Emmett and I talked about that once." They had had a conversation a year or so prior about where Peppermint Lightning actually came from and discussed the idea that there were other unseen forces in the universe as well.

"I doubt he mentioned this one. He may not have known about it. I know it was new to me, and it made him a little uneasy when he—I'll get to that. There is a force. It seems to be even older than Peppermint Lightning, or it . . . it feels that way, I suppose you might say. It . . . Well . . . if Peppermint Lightning is about joy and love, kindness and celebration, this other . . . it seems to be powered by fear."

"Fear?"

"I think so. I can't put my finger on it exactly."

"Chester, what aren't you telling me?"

"There is a man, he'd be older than your parents according to my records. He used to write to Santa every year. His letters were perfectly normal. He wanted toy trains, then army men and a bicycle. He asked for crayons and new pencils and notebooks when he got a little older."

"Okay." Sidney was trying to be patient because she knew Chester wouldn't be telling the story if it wasn't important, but it seemed to be taking a rather indirect route to helping Martin.

"But there was something about his letters that worried the chief. This man, Dale Connors—he was always on the nice list. He always left cookies."

"Respect."

"Indeed. But his letters unnerved Mr. Claus. He said there was an energy about them. When I asked him to explain, he trembled a little, the memory still clear, evidently. He said the boy's house was full of it too. There was Peppermint Lightning a'plenty, but there was this other, this pulsing other thing.

"You know Santa can't keep all the letters he gets. He tried. For years he tried, but as the world's population grew and Christmas spread, it became impossible. We do keep a tremendous volume, though. And we keep Dale's. They are kept in a room I'd never been in, and in the archives, that's unusual.

I asked Emmett to fetch them when he had a chance and he came back empty handed. He'd found them, but they'd turned his blood to ice and that's no easy feat when you're an elf."

"I imagine not. Did you go and get them?"

"I did. They are absolutely normal, but they pulse, they vibrate with an energy that stands your hairs on end . . . or I imagine it would, were I hairy. When you concentrate on them, it makes you imagine dark corners, low voices . . . ghosts and . . . other things."

"Okay. Okay. So, I think what you're getting at is this Dale character might have a connection to ghosts."

"He may. Or it may be to some other thing."

"And you think he may be able to help Martin."

"It is possible."

"Do you know anything else about him? Do you think he's dangerous?"

"I don't have any reason to suspect that, no. I can try to find current contact information and forward that to you, if you think it wise."

"I don't know if it's wise, but it sounds like it may be a place to start. I appreciate your help, Chester."

"It is always a pleasure, my dear. But, Sidney, be careful how close you get to this. There's something ancient here, something possibly dark, and I wouldn't want you—"

"You're sweet to worry, Chester, but I'll be careful. This one is on Martin, though. I'm just a . . . consultant, I suppose."

"Very well. We'll chat or I'll see you before you know it. Bye, love."

"Bye."

Sidney leaned back against her pillows, her lips pursed, brow furrowed. "Well, that got weird fast," she said to no one. Then her phone vibrated as Dale Connor's contact information came through.

* * *

"Dad, do you think the legend of Stingy Jack is real?"

"Okay. That came out of nowhere." Before Martin could decide how

9

to respond to the bizarre experience with the pumpkin, before he could formulate a plan or decide how to get involved, he wanted a little back story. His father was good with stories.

Donald Kelly was a professor of literature. He was always reading stories or telling one. He was also an amateur cryptozoologist, and you couldn't study Bigfoot or the chupacabra without delving into stories.

"There wasn't a lot written about him, Buster. It's considered folklore, and that means it was mostly a story people told each other; oral tradition. It gets passed down through the generations, most likely changing a little every time. Sooner or later someone writes it down and changes it again."

"But did it start with something real?"

"It could have. You know the story?"

"I've read about him. There was a thing on HalloweenVille about him last year."

"So, you know it has to do with conning the devil and being cursed, that kind of thing?"

"Yeah. I know. He got the devil to turn himself into a coin to pay his bar tab, then switched coins, and dropped the devil in his pocket. There was a cross in Jack's pocket and the devil was trapped. Eventually, he got free and cursed Jack to roam the darkness with only his little lantern; a coal in a turnip. "

"So, it's unlikely the story the way we know it is based in any kind of reality. There very well could have been a man named Jack who did some things people told stories about. Maybe he was a miserly trickster who earned a reputation and met with a strange end, but the rest of it . . . I guess we'll never know."

"I think he was a real person."

"He could have been."

"And he was Irish."

"Yes, that's where the story comes from."

"But . . . but there wouldn't be any records of him, would there? I mean, would there be any way to find out who the person actually was, or if he had a family?"

"No, I don't think so. Why? You think you'll find him in the family tree?"

Dad chuckled and slapped Martin on the shoulder.

"No. No, that's crazy. I was just curious."

"Well, curiosity is one of my favorite character traits. You could always do some research."

"I did. I asked you."

"No, I mean actual research, like reading books. Your great-grandad kept all kinds of books in his trunk. It's all up in the attic. I'm sure if you dig around in there, you'll find some version of the legend. Maybe you'll find old Stingy Jack in a family photo album." Dad gave Martin a sly grin.

"Research is what the internet is for. Besides, it's like school work. I have enough of that already."

"Speaking of—"

"Yes. It's done."

"Good man."

Martin hadn't gotten the answers he was hoping for. A part of him had really hoped his father would delve into a tale about their great ancestor and how he was misunderstood, and the story was really an unfair portrayal of some crazy event a couple hundred years ago. Unfortunately, he'd gotten no answers at all.

* * *

There was the faintest rustle of leaves. Only the most careful listeners would have heard a thing. That's how it was supposed to be. That's how a creature of shadows hunted. It's how a spy observed, undetected. It's how an intruder slipped in unnoticed.

Lilith was an expert hunter, a master spy, and a flawless secret invader. She jumped, crouched, jumped again, and was through the window without so much as disturbing the curtains. She slinked along behind the bar and sniffed the air. Her ears twitched.

"Oh, for the love of . . . Of all the bars in all the world! What are you doing here?"

Lilith leapt onto the bar and sat, staring Jack squarely in the eyes. "Looking for you, of course."

Cats, besides being expert hunters, are capable of slipping across the veil at will. They are creatures of both worlds whose keen eyes can see things humans cannot.

"Why? Why can't ye leave me in peace?" Jack said.

"Why can't you follow the rules? You aren't supposed to be here."

"I'm pretty sure cats aren't supposed to be in pubs. So, we'll both accept we're mixed up and you can go on your way."

Lilith stood and padded across the bar to Jack, rubbing her cheeks against the back of his hand.

"You know, cat, I thought one of the benefits of being dead and incorporeal was that yer kind wouldn't be able to do that anymore. What good is being made of dust and shadows if a bloomin' cat can still harass you?"

Lilith purred and continued to rub her cheeks on the spirit until he jerked his hand away.

"You know, they are probably looking for you."

"I'm sure they are," Jack replied.

"And sooner or later they will find you."

"They may, but I've beaten them before."

"*He* wasn't in charge then, though," Lilith said.

"No. He wasn't. But he doesn't scare me."

"He should."

Jack blew out a puff of air and shook his head. "You know I've been around longer than he has, don't you?"

"True, but he has ambition. He has purpose."

"And I—"

"And you're a spirit in a barroom. You can't drink. You can't eat."

"It helps me think."

"And what are you thinking about? Him?"

"No."

"Yes you are."

"I'm not."

"You are."

"You know, cats are obnoxiously persistent. If the living could hear you talk—"

"They can when I want them to."

"And when is that?"

"Almost never."

"Why can't I be so lucky?"

Lilith had hopped down from the bar and was slinking between Jack's feet, rubbing her sides just above his ankles.

"So," Lilith asked, "What are you doing here? Really? You know they'll be looking. You know they'll probably find you. It's only a matter of time. Are you working on a plan? Is it a good plan?"

"I don't know yet. I hope so. I'm looking for help."

"Help? On this side?"

"It's not unheard of."

"But it's unlikely," Lilith said.

"I have kin here."

"You have kin?"

"Why does everyone find that so hard to believe? Of course I do. I didn't have children of me own, but I had brothers and sisters. They had children. I was an uncle, a great-uncle many times over!"

"And one of these nieces or nephews lives here?"

"Aye."

"A long way from the old country."

"What do you know of the old country?"

Between purrs, Lilith replied, "Generational memory," as though she expected that to explain all.

"Bah!" Jack replied. "But, yes. A long way indeed. I had kin that settled here a hundred years after I first crossed the veil."

"And why this particular branch of the family tree?"

"He's the youngest."

"So?"

"That makes him the most suggestible."

Chapter 3

Martin read Sidney's message over and over again. It wasn't making sense to him, but Sidney had not been able to shed any additional light on it when he asked. There was some kind of force that existed in the realm of ghosts. This force scared the people who encountered it. There was a man who seemed, if not central to it, at least to be involved in a way neither he nor Sidney understood. He knew he had it jumbled, but wasn't even sure that straightening it out would help solve the problem Jack had presented him. But it gave him a place to start.

Martin tapped away at his phone, entering the name and contact information Sidney had given him. Dale Connors was an author. According to Martin's search results, he'd once written a couple of horror stories for a popular magazine Martin had a subscription to. He didn't appear to have made a career of storytelling, and there wasn't anything remarkable about him so far as Martin could tell. Sidney's contact said there *was* something remarkable, however, even if he didn't exactly understand what it was—and that made it a viable lead.

He needed to ask Jack about the man, should the spirit appear again. Martin assumed he was going to have to contact Mr. Dale Connors himself sooner or later. Jack's plight aside, Martin was hooked on the mystery of this force Sidney described, and he didn't think he'd be able to let it go.

"Mom, Dad, have you ever heard of Dale Connors?"

"No. Who is he?" Dad asked.

"He's a writer. He wrote horror stories for a magazine, probably when you were in college or maybe a little later."

"No. That wouldn't have been something I was interested in. I read a lot of fantasy and a healthy amount of science fiction back then. Honey? You read some horror and thriller stuff back then."

"Mom did?" Martin shot his mother a look, one eyebrow cocked.

Mom said, "A little, but mysteries have always been more my cup of tea."

"What brings up an obscure horror writer from way back in our youth?" Dad asked with a crooked grin.

"Oh, his name just came up when I was searching scary stories. I hadn't heard of him before is all."

Martin finished scooping Count Chocula from his bowl and polished off his orange juice as Dad buttered a couple pieces of toast and stuffed papers in his messenger bag. Dad never left himself enough time for breakfast, but always left enough time to get Martin his and chat a little before work. Mom would have a cup of tea and maybe some toast before ushering Martin off to the bus stop and leaving for work.

At the front door, Mrs. Kelly gave her husband a peck on the cheek before he left.

"Have a good day, honey," she said.

"You too, sweetheart. Love you."

"Love you, too."

The front door shut with a soft click, then Martin heard his father's car come to life and fade out of the driveway.

"You read horror back in the day?" Martin asked.

"Back in the day?'"

Martin smiled, "Yeah. You never read any of Dale Connor's stuff, though?"

"I read a few horror novels when I was younger, but not a lot of short stories, so I probably didn't see any of his material. Have you read them?"

"No. I haven't found them yet. His name came up in a list of things I might want to read."

"I could give you a few recommendations, you know."

"I'm not into whodunits, Mom."

"And your teacher isn't into horror, Buster. She might want to read a book report that isn't about the supernatural for once."

"Maybe, but Halloween isn't the time to change it up."

"I suppose that's true. After Halloween, it might be time to change it up a little, though. All that scary stuff isn't good for you. You about ready to go? It's supposed to be chilly today."

Martin reached into his backpack which rested slung across the back of his chair and produced his gloves and a hat. "It's not actually going to be chilly, mom. This weather has been lame for fall."

"Well, the weather channel says it's coming and it might drop today."

"And I packed this stuff in my bag so you didn't have to tell me to."

"It won't do you any good in your bag."

"You're such a mom," Martin replied.

"It's kind of my job," she said. She switched off the coffee pot, and they headed out the door together.

* * *

Jack had places to visit. As a spirit, it was easier to get around than it had been during his life—not as easy as when he first crossed over, but it still beat walking or horseback. He'd slipped through to the villages and towns, cities and neighborhoods of his kin over the years, searching for places full of haunted history and eerie legends. The New England region of the United States had been the most plentiful. Jack had searched these lands for places where he could thrive, leeching off the fear and wonder of the most fabled and folklore-saturated locals.

There was a cemetery in Concord, Massachusetts, a town square in Salem, a lighthouse in Maine, and a coastal tourist city in Rhode Island that offered respite and relative safety. There were people ripe for a scare, a spook, a trick, and that was all he needed. With All Hallows approaching, it was easier than usual. That made New England prime real estate to establish a refuge. It also made it a likely entry point for the coming invasion. Jack sat and leaned back against a gnarled tree in the Sleepy Hollow cemetery, the irony of his chosen location not lost on him in the least.

"You know," Lilith said, slinking her way around the trunk of the tree to

16

hop on Jack's lap, "He's not from here. His Sleepy Hollow is in upstate New York."

Jack swept the cat aside. "I know that. Why are you here?"

"I followed you."

"I can see that. Why?"

"You're interesting."

"Well, then I need to try to be more boring."

Jack stood, mostly to evict Lilith from his lap, and wandered the cemetery. In that particular area, some of the grave markers were nearly as old as he was—or at least closer to his age than most of the cemeteries this side of the Atlantic. It wasn't a terribly spooky place, not a lot of tales of haunted graves or things going bump in the night, but it was old enough that it felt familiar, close enough to his kind that he could travel without expending much energy, and far enough from home that it wasn't a painful place to visit.

Home was a place of regret, a place where he was reminded of the tricks he'd played and the people he'd cheated. Ireland was a reminder he'd not been close to his family and the place he'd played the trick which ultimately doomed him to his fate.

"You come up with a plan?" Lilith asked, jogging through the leaves alongside his path."

"Not that it's your concern, but, yes. Although only the very beginnings of one."

"What is it?"

Jack sighed. "Well, I'm going to tell him the truth."

Have you ever heard a cat laugh? It starts with a little smirk, a little upturn of the lips, a little widening in the eyes and is followed by a sound somewhere between a hiccup and hairball. Jack had heard the sound before and he didn't appreciate it any more now than he had the other times.

"It's a fact, cat." Jack said sourly. "The only way to get him started is to tell him the score."

"And then?"

"Well—"

Lilith interrupted. "That's your whole plan, isn't it? Your plan is to tell him a story and let him figure out the rest. How old is this kin of yours? How is he going to help?"

Jack refused to answer. He knew if he told the cat the truth, she'd ridicule him further and he could do well enough without it. "Why don't you come up with a plan then, puss?"

"You know I hate being called that?"

"Oh, you do? So sorry about that."

"I don't need a plan. I'd rather see things remain the way they are, of course, but it's up to you lot to make a difference," Lilith said.

"I suppose I'll ask the next raven I see then. They'll have something useful to add."

Lilith stopped walking and spat. "Ravens!" she said, a bitterness in her tone that made Jack glad the barb had stuck.

"Sure. There are bound to be some around here somewhere."

"Don't you dare."

"You know, the man who brought ravens to their fame once lived—"

"Jack, I'm warning you. We're friends and I would hate to tear into you, but spirits can still be scratched and bitten, you know."

Jack smiled, satisfied, and said no more.

Chapter 4

Martin had no idea if it would work. There was nothing about it that said that it would, only that it should. By supernatural fiction law, it all made sense. He'd carried the pumpkin out into the woods. He was exceptionally glad to have woods within a short bike ride from the house. Cruising down the road with a pumpkin in his backpack would not only attract curiosity but was uncomfortable. And heavy. He'd decided that he couldn't carve the pumpkin first. It wouldn't survive the journey. He couldn't come up with an excuse to be out of the house at midnight, so twilight was going to have to work. That time of year, it comes early and he could be home before it was too dark. He wouldn't beat the streetlights, but it was an easy, safe ride home and it hadn't been too difficult to convince his parents he could stay out just a little longer.

"Shadowy woods? Check. Carved pumpkin? Working on it," he said to himself. His mother hadn't had any black candles. He wasn't especially surprised by that. He'd had to settle for a dark red one he dug from a box of Christmas things in the garage. He'd snatched a long-reach charcoal grill lighter from the garage as well. Martin also opted against pentagrams, incantations, and had only very briefly entertained the idea of spilling a few drops of his own blood, the blood of Jack's kin supposedly.

The pumpkin was carved into a sneer. A smile didn't seem right and a fanged, frightful, or angry face seemed to send the wrong signal. The candle was set into place and lit. Martin sat a few feet from it, legs crossed, pumpkin guts and seeds piled in the grass nearby, attracting a few flies.

"Okay," Martin said to himself. "Okay."

He sat and stared at the flame. It was still light enough that the face of the pumpkin didn't have much of a glow, so he stared up towards the half-moon becoming more and more distinct in the evening sky.

It took a great deal of convincing himself not to abandon the idea within the first few minutes after sitting. It felt utterly ridiculous. Once he'd actually set the stage he realized he looked like a lunatic and if he tried to explain to anyone passing by, there was no false story he could tell that would sound any more sane than the real one.

Ten minutes that felt like an hour passed. Martin looked around the woods, shadows growing long. He listened. It was quiet. A few birds called. He could hear cars on the street a few hundred yards away.

"This is ridiculous," he said aloud.

"It is. Yes. I respect the effort though, lad. It wasn't a bad plan. I wish I could tell you that a little of me exists in each lantern lit in each gourd across North America and Europe, that I can feel the tug of someone searching for me in that flame, but I was actually headed this way, anyway. That is a nice face on that pumpkin, though. It supposed to be your great-great-uncle Jack?"

Martin jerked to look over his left shoulder. A pale, semitransparent form had approached him from behind.

To a cat, a raven, or anyone from beyond the veil, Jack appeared corporeal. On the mortal side, though, he got to decide if he had any shape at all—provided he had the energy. A foggy, vaguely man-shaped mist was all he was willing to spend the energy on at the moment. He'd considered appearing as a light in the pumpkin again to honor Martin's effort. That would have taken less energy. But he needed to have a grave conversation with the boy and thought a human form might be a better bearer of ill tidings than a flickering candle flame.

"Jack!" Martin said and rose quickly to his feet. "It is you, right?"

"Yes, lad. It is I."

* * *

"Were you looking for me?" Jack asked.

"Yes. I . . . uh . . . well, I want to know more. Why do you need help? How did you find me? Why me? What am I supposed to do to help you? Why should I help you?" Martin was counting off the questions by raising a finger on his left hand for each one.

"Those are a lot of questions. The answers for some are more important than others, if I'm being honest. And I came here—"

"Are you?" Martin asked.

"Here?" Jack asked.

"No. Honest. That isn't your reputation, you know." A black cat sauntered up from seemingly nowhere to wind itself through Jack's legs. It purred and rubbed itself along his ankles, then made its way to Martin. Evidently, Lilith hadn't wanted the boy to hear her, but Jack heard the, "Smart boy," between the purrs.

"Hi, kitty," Martin said, leaning down to scratch Lilith between the ears, eliciting an enthusiastic purr. "Where did you come from, huh?" He scratched under her chin and Jack answered the question.

"The underworld."

Martin cocked his head and looked quizzically at Jack.

"The underworld. That's where she came from," Jack said.

Lilith stopped purring and sat on her haunches, blinking at Jack.

"You know this cat? Is she yours?"

"No! Well, yes, I know her, but she is certainly not my cat. Lad, you'll find that cats don't belong to anyone. They don't belong to any place for that matter. They're irritating beasts from a realm where the solitary purpose of each living creature is to frustrate the skin off every being in this world and all the others."

"Wow," Martin said. "That's dramatic."

Lilith purred again and strutted around Martin, then around Jack, and came to a pause at the jack-o'-lantern. She sat and licked the back of a forepaw, which she then ran across her face a few times. She looked Martin directly in the eye and said, "It was. Wasn't it? Stingy here has a bit of flair for the dramatic you'll find; well, at least when that drama is complaining."

Martin backed up a few steps out of sheer instinctive response.

"Yeah. It talks," Jack said.

"We all do," Lilith replied. "All cats, I mean. We usually choose not to. Most of the time, if we have something to say, we whisper it while you aren't looking at us. Sometimes it gets through and sometimes it doesn't. Spirits we converse with freely."

Martin couldn't speak.

"And we wish they wouldn't," Jack said.

"And why did you follow me here this evening, puss?" Jack asked.

"I gathered you have a story to tell. I wanted to hear it. I do like stories and you are a pretty good teller." In truth, Lilith had followed Jack to see if he really was going to tell his distant-nephew the truth like he'd claimed. She hadn't decided if she would intervene if he didn't.

"I do indeed have a story to tell, and Martin m'lad had quite a few questions. I think my yarn will wrap them all up nicely."

* * *

"On the other side, you have all these worlds, and you can cross between them easily. This world, yours and once mine, is different. There is a barrier that separates them." Jack had been through it with Martin once already but was reviewing it because the boy seemed so struck by it that Jack wasn't sure he was processing it all correctly.

"And it's fear that powers this barrier?"

"More or less, yes."

"So fear is good? We want the barrier up?" Martin asked.

"Yes and no. You certainly don't want the other side to come rampaging in and take over your world. Your fears feed them and increase the power of those who want it most. Your fear makes them stronger. But, a healthy curiosity, a little spook, a scary story, the right amount of fear keeps the balance. We should enjoy some fear on this side—or be afraid of the right sorts of things."

Martin asked, "What are the right things to be afraid of?"

"There needs to be a balance, lad. If mortal man isn't afraid, all the power of fear becomes available to those on the other side of the barrier. When Halloween was scarier, when people wandered their neighborhoods and were spooked by friends, when people tapped on the veil in séances or went ghost hunting, or told scary tales these things made use of fear. As people became less curious and less afraid, the other side gathered power. People stopped dabbling in the things that kept the balance and are instead afraid of each other. It's a darker fear and one that the denizens of the other side desperately want to get their hands on. It will increase their power."

"Balance?" Martin asked.

"He's not even sure he understands it, Martin. He knows there is a battle coming—"

"It won't be a battle. This side will be overrun," Jack said.

"There is to be an invasion. The barrier must be strengthened or there will be nothing stopping him—them—from crossing," Lilith explained.

"Wait. You said 'him.' Is there someone specific trying to break through?"

Jack rubbed his face with his hands, a human gesture that looked strange coming from a phantom, and said, "There are lots of forces gathered, but they do have a leader. There is a spirit—once a man who's whipped them into a frenzy and convinced them they can break through."

"Who? Who is it?" said Martin.

Lilith answered, "The headless horseman."

Martin blinked. Then he shook his head a little and said, "The headless horseman . . . *the* headless horseman is leading an army of devils and ghosts to take over our world. This is nuts!"

"Nuts or not, we need to strengthen the barrier and keep him—them, at bay."

"And how do we do that?"

"We need more power on this side."

"How do we do *that*? Scare people?"

"Maybe. We need to . . . we need to spark those fears that keep things in balance," Jack said.

Lilith added, "He also doesn't know exactly how that's supposed to be done. He's hoping you will."

"So, you need my help sparking this power."

Jack nodded and Lilith swished her tail.

"I think I may know how to do that."

Lilith's ear perked up. Jack said, "You do?" with more surprise than he'd intended.

"The beginning of one, anyway. I asked a friend. You told me to find help. I did. And she pointed me in a direction that didn't make sense at the time, but it sort of does now." Martin had blown out the candle in the lantern and put it and his carving tools back in his backpack. The sun was barely still over the horizon. "Let me work on it. I have to get home."

"Wait. What are you going to do?" Jack asked.

"Like I said, I'm going to work on it. I don't even know if I'm on the right track."

"We don't have a lot of time. The veil is already weaker this time of year than usual, and with All Hallow's—"

"I get it." He hopped on his bike, put one foot on a pedal and said, "So, I don't need to go through all this again to reach you?" He tilted his head towards the pumpkin guts.

"No."

Lilith pawed at Jack's legs, an odd sight to Martin who could not see for certain that Jack *had* legs. "I have the best idea!" Jack said. "The cat can stay with you. She seems to always be able to find me, so if you make progress and need to reach me, she can find me—unfortunately."

"See," Lilith said. "I knew you loved me."

Jack snorted.

"My parents won't let me keep you, Lilith."

"That's okay. I'm a bit of a nomad anyway. I wouldn't object if you wanted to sneak a treat out for me, or leave a little blanket somewhere though."

"I'll tuck something under the porch for you. There's a place where the lattice is broken. A raccoon got down there once."

Lilith's hackles went up. "I'll run it off."

"You know where I live?" Martin asked. "Or are you going to follow me home?"

"I'll follow, but don't worry if you get too far ahead. I'll find the way. I've got better eyes and ears than you, after all."

"Fair enough. Later, Jack."

Jack shot Lilith a sidelong glance that she flatly ignored, then he faded from sight. Martin pedaled towards home, anxious to beat the moon to stay on the right side of his parents.

Chapter 5

Heavy hooves hammered the cold, dark ground. The great, black beast paced back and forth a dozen yards or so. It was unusual for the rider to visit the guardian of the veil. Messengers were easy enough to come by; spirits, wolves, cats, and of course ravens. The fact that the rider had come in person was not a good sign to anyone who happened to be near the veil.

He almost never dismounted. Few could recollect seeing the rider off of his horse. When he rode, his eyes blazed from the black holes of his pumpkin head. When his horse slowed or came to rest, the flame diminished and he tucked his head under one arm. It was hard to be sure where his voice came from when he spoke, but it mattered little. It was a raspy, rumbling voice which commanded attention. It sounded like anger, like resentment, like hate, and it was not a voice you wanted directed toward you.

"He crossed again, did he?" the headless horseman asked.

"Yes, he did."

"And how did you let that happen?"

"I was tricked."

"The Keeper of the Gate is so easily fooled? Then perhaps another should have your post."

"I've been here quite a long time, rider, and I suspect I will be here a great deal longer."

"You might not be required much longer, guardian. Tell me, how did Jack escape?"

"He is a trickster. His pranks, even his weaker seeming ones, have a way of succeeding. Maybe he is gifted."

"Are you saying you aren't to be held accountable?"

"No. He slipped past me and that is a failing on my part. I will deal with him when he returns."

"I see. This isn't the first lapse. Perhaps if you had dealt with him properly in the past—"

"For as long as there has been need for one, I have been the veil's guardian. Few have moved between these worlds who were not permitted."

"I need to know what this is about. There is a reason he's slipped through." He no longer appeared to be speaking to the guardian, but rather to himself. He hoisted the gourd back atop his shoulders and his eyes blazed once more. He turned his attention to the guardian. "Not another mistake. I can find ways to make you regret your incompetence." He kicked his horse and was off, back into the black wood.

* * *

The rider pulled his steed to a halt once he was deep enough into the woods he could hear the ravens' calls. "You know Jack of the Lantern," he shouted.

A chorus of caws answered.

"I need to know what he is about. He's slipped through the veil and walks among the mortals. See what he is doing and return to me."

Croaking voices echoed through the trees from all around him. Once settled, the collection of voices called back, "You do not rule this world, Bones! We do not answer to you."

The flames in the rider's eyes flared.

"You may wield fear with some, rider, but we are not afraid. Perhaps we will spy on Stingy Jack and perhaps we will not. Should we, it will be to satisfy our own curiosity. Perhaps we will share what we learn and perhaps we will not. Should we, it will be of our own decision."

The rider, once known in the mortal world as Brom Bones, lifted the pumpkin from his shoulders and hurled it into the trees whereupon it exploded and flames cascaded, causing the shadows to dance and ravens in the branches to take wing before resting again on others a little higher up.

"Temper now," the voices called.

The rider once again kicked his horse and raced off down the path, a burning glow arising from where a neck ought to be as a new head began to take form.

Chapter 6

Martin had his work cut out for him. There wasn't a school holiday, not so much as a three-day weekend coming up, and yet he had to convince his parents there was a good reason for them to travel to Maine. It was imperative, he'd decided, to see Dale Connors.

Based on what Martin read, the man was reclusive. He had no social media presence. Martin had only the contact information Sidney sent him, and he couldn't be sure it was current. He knew what the author's house looked like from a photo taken for an "about the author" blurb that accompanied one of the magazine stories, assuming he was still living in the same house. With the help of Google maps street view, he'd been able to zero in on what he felt confident was the right neighborhood. The only way to reach him was to find him in person.

"Mom, I had an idea for Dad's birthday," Martin told his mother as they emptied the dishwasher together.

"Buster, his birthday isn't until January."

"I know, but there's this thing coming up this weekend that I think he'd really enjoy. I thought maybe we could take him as an early present."

"What thing?"

"It's a Bigfoot thing in Maine."

"A Bigfoot thing?"

"Well, it's a cryptozoology thing, like a convention I guess. There are some speaker panels like at a comic-con, and one of them has some local experts on Sasquatch."

"He would like that, wouldn't he?"

Martin had hunted for some reason to entice at least one of his parents to go to Maine. He'd been lucky to find this particular event, though it was about an hour from Dale's home town. He was even luckier his mother seemed to be taking the bait.

"Yeah. It lasts all weekend. I thought maybe if we got him tickets and we all went up and spent the weekend—"

"I don't know if a weekend getaway is really in the budget right now, Buster. The holidays are coming up and—"

"I know. But this convention doesn't come around all the time." Martin had no idea if that was true or not, but it strengthened his argument. "And I really want to do something nice for him. I've just gotten him sweaters, or ties, or books for the last forever years. This would be great and it's something we could do as a family."

His mother smiled and nodded. Let me think it over. It's this weekend?"

"Yeah." Martin couldn't believe his ploy seemed to be working, but that was only step one. It got him to the right state, but it didn't get him to Dale's house. That part of the plan came next. He'd considered suggesting some kind of detour but couldn't find a single reason for them to go to Pineborough where Dale lived, so it was going to take something else.

* * *

Martin wasn't sure what Sidney would or could do with what he'd learned, but felt she'd want to know and he was eager to share it with someone.

She was glad he did. She was genuinely, enthusiastically interested.

Wow, Martin. You've got yourself a seriously cool mystery to solve, maybe even some world-saving stuff. I'm jealous.

You did a bit of it yourself, he replied.

I don't know. I mean, I realize I helped. I made a difference, and I think it was an important one, but you're talking about an invasion of the dead, the undead, the—what all are we talking about?

I don't even know for sure, but enough that it's safe to say we want to stop it. I just have to figure out how and come up with a plan to get from the convention we're taking my dad to, to this author's house. I'm at a loss there.

There was a pause before messenger chimed with a reply.

I think I can help with that.

You can? Martin was incredulous. *How?*

Well, I have an idea but I don't want to jinx it by telling you now. I'll reach out to a friend and see what we can do. If it works, I'll give you a heads up. It might be a good idea to keep brainstorming, but I have a feeling this friend of mine will chomp at the chance to lend a hand to something like this.

Sidney knew exactly who to ask for help. She was thinking of a particular friend who was almost certain to agree to look after Martin and assist where she could.

I'll keep thinking. Let me know what you find out, Martin said.

I sure will. Keep me posted if anything else weird happens.

You mean like if the barrier between worlds collapses and we're overrun by the spirits of Valhalla and Hades?

Yeah. That kind of thing. She finished with a winking face emoji and signed off.

Chapter 7

Mom had consented, under the condition that they not tell Martin's father where they were going.

"Don't even ask," she said. "It is a surprise your son came up with and you're going to love it."

Dad turned around in the passenger seat to face his son. He grinned and nodded. "Buster, I have no idea what you're up to, but I appreciate your thoughtfulness."

They had booked a hotel in South Portland, Maine. It was just past leaf-peeping season, so the room rates were more reasonable than Martin's mom thought they would be. That had probably been what clinched the deal. They'd set off about eight in the morning. They'd arrive at the convention a little after ten. That was early enough to get the lay of the land, check the speaker schedule and get some lunch before the afternoon's key events. Martin's mom had done some searching on Yelp for a restaurant she thought her husband would enjoy. He was a sucker for seafood, especially a lobster roll, and it was still the right season for them.

Sidney had sent Martin a somewhat cryptic message late the night before, and they had a brief conversation which set his mind at ease about getting to Dale's house but also gave him a little anxiety.

"All set. A friend will get you there. It's unconventional, but you'll be in good hands. Be outside your hotel as soon as you can after dark. She'll find you."

"She?"

"Trust me, you won't miss her. I don't want to spoil the surprise, though. I think you're going to love it."

* * *

Mom had opted for route 1A instead of interstate 95. Even with most of the leaves now brown or on the ground it was a far more scenic route. Martin's father had always enjoyed the drive and he knew all kinds of history about the coastal towns along the way. Martin had heard it often enough that he wasn't tuned in as his father shared the stories again. Instead, he was reading.

He'd found archived copies of Dale's stories and was doing what he considered to be research by reading them. The stories themselves didn't blow the doors off the horror genre, but Martin had read much worse. Even without a great story, though, there was something about Dale's work that seemed to crackle. Maybe he was imagining it. Thinking about what Sidney had told him made him conjure something that wasn't really there. He did find himself wishing there were more of them. He also wished he wasn't going to be alone on that part of the trip.

He would have with him, he assumed, whoever Sidney was sending to help, but the experts on the situation weren't going to be there. Jack hadn't turned up since their meeting in the forest earlier in the week and he'd spotted Lilith in the back yard as they were getting ready to leave that morning, but for all intents and purposes, he was on his own with Dale and he wasn't feeling especially confident about it.

They drove without conversation for a while; road noise and NPR's morning classical programming filling the silence. Martin read the few things he could find written by Dale, then moved to reading several versions of the Stingy Jack story. When he'd read enough they were starting to repeat, he did a few searches and read a few articles about other worlds. Most of what he found under those search terms involved quantum theory about parallel dimensions. Though interesting, Martin deemed them not relevant to his mission.

He did find a few articles that talked about the nine worlds of Norse mythology and wondered if all nine of those worlds existed beyond the much-discussed veil. He searched again, exchanging "worlds" for "realms" and did a little better. This search returned results about several versions of afterlife destinations, the realm of Fae, the realm of magic—which seemed to be a generic term for things people couldn't explain with science, and then a lot of fantasy fiction. He picked up interesting bits and pieces, but nothing that got him any closer to a solution.

He tried, not expecting any useful returns, a search on the veil or the barrier between worlds. He got results from science websites having to do with black holes but there also were a surprising number of blog posts, and what might be pseudoscience or new-age websites, about spirits crossing between worlds, demons, possession—supposedly mythical creatures sneaking from one side of the veil to the other.

Folklore, older stories from all over the world, existed, in which it was commonplace for creatures not of the mortal world of humans to visit and sometimes bring people back to other places, other worlds. These legends, fairy tales, and myths took on a new meaning for Martin on that car ride.

"Is it possible it's all real?" he asked himself. "A place where souls are tortured, a land of dragons and unicorns, leprechauns, a paradise full of angels, places where dead warriors feasted, frost giants roamed, a place of epic battles between fallen heroes, a place where elves—" He stopped himself there. Elves were real. He knew that. Sidney knew elves personally. If they were real couldn't the rest of it be too? If cats could talk and spirits could haunt jack-o'-lanterns, was the rest of it real too?

He opened the messaging app on his phone once more and sent Sidney a question. "Have elves always lived in this world or are they from one of the other worlds Jack told me about?"

He didn't get an answer right away. He checked his phone obsessively. Whatever the answer, it didn't have much bearing on what he was in the middle of, but it would lend some proof that he wasn't being fooled altogether. "After all," he thought, "tricks are Jack's standard."

* * *

They arrived in South Portland and made their way to the hotel where the convention was being held. It wasn't the cheapest hotel in the area, but it was the most convenient, and it had a pool and hot tub—and Mom had found a good deal on it. "Isn't it too early to check in?" Dad asked.

Mom smiled. "It is, but we aren't checking in just yet." Dad cocked his head and Mom pointed to the marquee below the hotel's brand sign.

"Welcome Crypto-Con."

"Oh my god," Dad said. "You brought me to a—"

"Yep," Martin said. He was genuinely pleased to see his father's reaction, but the satisfaction came wrapped in guilt. He wouldn't have found the place or suggested they come without ulterior motives. "There are some cool panels and guest speakers and it's only happening this weekend."

"He talked you into this?" Dad asked Mom.

"He was very convincing."

Dad replied, "You know, I think we have raised a fine young man."

Mom smiled. She'd pulled the car into a spot not far from the front doors, and Dad practically jumped out.

"Buster," Mom said, "we'll have a hard time keeping up with your father."

"That's okay," Martin replied. "There's a cafe here. And after we check in, we can always rest in the room."

"Nope. This trip was your idea. You have to keep up with Dad. I can go relax in the pool."

"The pool?" Martin asked.

"I packed your trunks, don't worry."

"You know, Dad, I think I've got a pretty good mom here."

* * *

The convention floor had maybe a couple dozen booths arranged along opposite walls, and there was an information and check-in desk just inside the front doors. It wasn't a massive hall, like you might see in a big city comic-con. It was a large banquet and meeting room, but the look on his father's face said it could have been Main Street, USA in Disney World.

Some of the booths were elaborate with large posters, banners, or bunting and two or three tables covered in literature, video monitors and glass cases presumably full of artifacts collected by crypto-researchers. Other booths were single folding tables with pamphlets or a few stacks of books.

There was merchandise everywhere, too. There were t-shirts, baseball caps, posters, key chains, and patches at nearly all the booths. Only the smaller ones seemed to be without racks of things for sale, and even those had bumper stickers or pins.

Martin took it all in from the doorway as his parents checked in and Mom paid the admission which earned them wristbands with a camouflage pattern on them. As fascinating as it all was, there were two thoughts running through Martin's mind, competing for dominance over his attention. First, he wondered if all these creatures were real. Given what he'd learned, was it possible the moth man and grass man, Nessie and Bigfoot, the Jersey devil and all the rest were as real as Jack and all the things from his stories? He'd never believed any of it. He knew his father did, or at least wanted to, but Martin had never seen any convincing evidence. He supposed that might change today.

His other thought was the same one he'd had since leaving that morning. He wondered what he was going to do when he got to Dale's house, assuming he made it there. And it wasn't just that, but what he was doing at all. The car ride from Massachusetts to Maine had provided a lot of quiet time. Even his reading was distracted by the growing thought that this was all a little too much. He considered the possibility he was losing his mind, but then there was Sidney. Not only had they talked about it, Sidney herself was proof of there being more to the world than meets the eye. If her experiences weren't crazy, maybe his weren't either. If they weren't, that still left him with the problem of figuring out what to do about it. How was he, a fourteen-year-old kid from Carlisle, Massachusetts supposed to defeat the forces of darkness or hordes of the dead even with the help of a reclusive, unsuccessful author?

Ultimately, he had decided all he could do was go with it. He hoped it would be a little clearer once he'd met Dale, but in the meantime all he could do was accept this was his reality, and move forward. It didn't do any good to worry about the clock ticking away. With any luck, he'd figure it out before his world was overrun. Martin had been lost so deeply in these thoughts he hadn't noticed his father talking to him until he felt his dad's hand on his shoulder. "You okay there, Buster?"

"Yeah. Yeah. Sorry. I was just taking it all in."

"Me too! This is great. Thanks a bunch. Where should we start, left side or right side? The panels I want to hear are in another room and they aren't until later this afternoon, so we have plenty of time to wander the floor. What do you say?"

"I don't know, Dad. This is your day. You lead the way."

Martin's mother enjoyed her husband's enthusiasm, though she had no interest in cryptozoology herself. The fervor of the event was all a little too much for her. Some of the attendees took their hobby a little too seriously, in her opinion, and their intensity, combined with sensory overload from all the booth operators vying for attention, she opted to leave the boys after visiting the third stall.

"Gentlemen," she said. "I'm going to the lounge and see if I can scare up a cup of tea. I'll come back and find you in a little while. Take your time. Enjoy yourselves. We'll grab some lunch when I come back."

"Okay, dear," Martin's father said and gave his wife a peck on the cheek.

"Okay, Mom," Martin said. She headed out of the banquet hall. As she walked off, Martin turned halfway around to wave at her, half expecting her to embarrass him by blowing a kiss. A booth across the aisle caught his eye. A glossy black banner hung over the table which read, "Creatures from Another World?" and a chill ran up his spine.

Chapter 8

Mrs. Kelly checked the family into their room and after enjoying the hotel's amenities for a while, found a restaurant offering take-out and returned laden with dinner to the hotel room early that evening.

With a full day's event schedule behind them, tired feet, and bellies full of lobster rolls, Martin and his parents settled into their room. They didn't have to bother with unpacking since they only had the one night, but Mom liked to settle in so she put their clothes in a drawer and toiletries on the sink. Dad kicked off his shoes and lay back in one of the two queen beds with the TV remote. Mom went into the bathroom to change.

"So, everyone had fun today?" she called from behind the closed door.

"I did," Martin said.

"Oh, it was great. Some of these people have really done their research! And in one of the panels we went to, a guy showed some really compelling new still shots of what appears to be a sasquatch in central New Hampshire."

Mom said, "Wow," though Martin and his father knew she wasn't really impressed.

"There was this one guy," Martin added, "that said that a Bigfoot spent a weekend in his garage. He had hair in this little glass case he'd been trying to get some genetics lab in Boston to analyze. He had casts of footprints too."

Dad scoffed. "You see that all the time. The casts looked faked to me, and the man never saw a Bigfoot. He just heard something and found hair samples. These guys that try to fake evidence really hurt the reputation of people trying to do legitimate research."

Mom emerged from the bathroom in a set of matching flannel pajamas with an autumn leaf pattern on them. She settled in next to her husband in bed. Martin wasn't sure where to go from there.

He couldn't very well walk out the door just then. His parents had only just unwound. He had no good excuse to head back out. They had stuffed themselves recently enough that a snack run to the vending machines wasn't believable. He changed into his own pj's while his dad did the same.

The sun had disappeared beyond the horizon, though it hadn't grown entirely dark yet. He didn't know who or what was going to be waiting for him, but he didn't want to keep them waiting. He didn't end up having a choice. He waited through a rerun of an episode of Survivorman and his father drifted off. He wasn't snoring yet, but Martin thought he would be soon. His mother was still awake with no immediate signs of slipping off. He couldn't think of a single reason he could use to leave the room, and even if he had, his mother would have waited for him to return before she closed her eyes.

Mom watched most of a documentary on the Science Channel about rainforests in South America, Martin pretending to sleep all the while before she finally appeared to nod off. He waited just a little longer to be sure, then climbed out of bed and changed back into his clothes as silently as he could. He grabbed his father's room key from the nightstand, put on his jacket and paused at the door. He thought if his parents woke up and he was missing it might go badly. They might panic. He didn't know how long he'd be gone. He couldn't be gone all night. His parents would find him missing in the morning and after calling the hotel manager, they would call the police.

He grabbed the complimentary hotel notepad and pen and jotted a quick note. "I couldn't sleep. Too excited. I took Dad's key and I'm going to take a walk around the hotel. I have my phone. Love you."

That would at least buy him a little leeway. If they woke up, read the note, and he wasn't back soon after, it would come unraveled quickly. The best he could hope for was a quick trip. Well, he hoped for a quick trip, Dale being home, Dale answering the door, them having a productive conversation in which they figured out how to save the world, and a swift silent return to his hotel bed.

Martin rode the elevator to the ground floor, his heart hammering in his chest. He walked down the hall to the back door of the building and stepped out into the chilly night air. It wasn't late, but at that time of year it might as well have been midnight for the darkness. He stepped out onto the sidewalk and looked up and down the parking lot for anything that appeared out of place. He looked for a woman waiting in a car or truck. Sidney had said "she."

He scanned, looking to the edge of the parking lot where it met the woods to see if there was anyone in the shadows. He couldn't see a thing. Anxiety was quickly giving way to disappointment and something like despair when he heard a whisper.

"Martin. Psst. Martin, if that's you, step over here into the woods. Sidney sent me."

Martin nearly leapt off the curb.

"Don't run, hon. You'll attract suspicion. Besides, you got to look both ways." The voice had a vaguely southern accent. It was low and warm sounding, even in a whisper. Martin slowed his pace, though he still hadn't bothered to look both ways across the parking lot, and took a few steps into the woods. He still didn't see anyone.

Then he heard a snort and saw tendrils of vapor like the ones produced by his own breath. Out from behind an eastern white pine, several yards further into the shadows, stepped an animal he'd never seen in person before. He knew right away what it was, even without jingle bells or a sleigh harnessed to it.

"Pleasure to meet you, sugah. I'm Baxter."

"Baxter?" Martin was surprised he could even form the word.

"Yes, sir. Not expecting a reindeer, I gather?"

"I wasn't sure what to expect, but—"

"It wasn't me?"

Martin just stared. He supposed that after talking to Lilith as he had, a talking reindeer should not have been as big a shock as it was.

"Don't worry. I don't take any offense. Reindeer aren't native to Maine, though I must say I've always liked the climate. You ready to go?"

"You know where we're going?"

"I sure do. I have the coordinates, so to speak. I've swung by already and it looks like your author is at home. Climb on." She folded her front legs under her and knelt down.

"You want me to . . . I'm going to . . ."

"Unless you want to walk beside me. But I think this will be much quicker. Don't worry, you aren't going to hurt me any, and I promise I won't let you get hurt. All you have to do is swing one leg over to the other side and hold on around my neck."

"Okay," Martin said and cautiously climbed on Baxter's back. "Um, we aren't flying are we? I mean, that's what you do, right?"

"Well, we're going to have to do a little of that, yes. Don't worry, I'm a flying ace. We'll gallop along a little first until you get your balance, though. Hold on, hon."

* * *

"He's not going to answer the door! This guy is known for being a recluse."

"Surely he'll at least come and see who it is."

"He won't. I'm sure of it. If I knock on the door or ring the bell, he might look and see who it is, but he certainly isn't going to open up."

"You aren't even going to try? Then what are we doing here, hon?"

Martin kicked at the dark mud under his feet. "I don't know. This is crazy."

"I won't disagree with you on that point, sugah, but it seems like if you've got to speak with this man, you need to get inside or . . ."

"Or what?" Martin cocked an eyebrow and looked at Baxter.

"Or we get him to come out."

"Go on."

"If we get him out here and he sees you aren't a late night Boy Scout selling popcorn or an energy company doing an after-hours survey, you might get a chance to talk to him."

Martin pursed his lips. "Well, that's possible. But how are we going to get him outside?"

Baxter pawed at the mud Martin had just kicked, leaned down low and sniffed the earth. "Follow me," she said, and took a few steps deeper into the woods. She kept pawing at the ground, sniffing, and kicking up mud with her front hooves. Martin followed in silence, too curious to interrupt.

Baxter stopped. "This man is all about his scary stories, right?"

"Yes. At least he was."

"And the supernatural? Monsters and the like?"

"Yes. So?" said Martin.

"So, do you think a monster coming right up to his gate would get him out of his house?"

Martin shrugged, rubbed his face with both hands and said, "I don't know. It might. It might also get him to lock the doors and call the police."

"I don't think so. I think he'd be too intrigued. And if he's as reclusive as you say, he's not likely to call anyone and draw attention. I think he'd investigate."

"Okay. But where are we going to find a monster? I mean, my whole thing right now is stopping monsters from showing up."

Baxter kicked hard into the earth, first with one front hoof and then the other. A wet, black gout of mud erupted around her. "We're going to make one. Stand back, sugah."

In a way far more similar to a dog digging for bones than Martin would have thought a reindeer could manage, Baxter churned the earth. Her great hooves made short work of the soil and it was churned into a thick, sticky soup of mud, pine needles, and decaying leaves in a matter of minutes.

She turned the earth over in this way in an area of about ten feet by six feet, then looked at Martin and said, "You're going to want to step back a few more feet, I think."

With that, she dropped to her side and rolled around in the muck, grinding and squirming in the slop until it covered her left side from neck to tail. She kicked her legs in the air and rolled to the other side, repeating the process. Martin gaped. Baxter rose, mud dripping from every quarter, bits of broken sticks, small stones, dead leaves, and clumps of pine needles ground into her thick fur. "Now," she said, "Do my neck and head."

Martin didn't hesitate. He scooped up handfuls of the dark earth and smeared them up Baxter's neck, under her chin, over the back of her head and down her face.

"Don't be shy, hon. Get it all over."

Martin applied more mud and daubed it all over her muzzle and snout. He stuffed some pine needles and leaves in it for good measure.

"How do I look?" Baxter asked.

Martin stepped back. He scratched his chin the way his father did when he was growing a short beard and said, "Well . . . I'm not sure you're all that terrifying, but from a distance, if I didn't know what you were, I'd have questions. It needs something, though."

Martin unslung his backpack and set it on the ground. He unzipped the front pouch and pulled out two small foil packages. He opened the largest pouch and dug around until he found two more, these long and narrow.

"These will help," he said, turning back to the filthy, sodden reindeer.

"Whatcha got there?"

"My mom doesn't let me leave the house when it gets dark early like it does this time of year, without a little illumination." He opened the first pouch and pulled out a green glow stick. He snapped it and shook it, and the sickly greenish glow began to brighten. He did the same with the second small pouch. Then, from the other two, he removed long glow necklaces in the same sickly yellow green. He snapped the glow toys to life. Baxter cocked her long head towards him and made a snuffling sound Martin took for curiosity.

"We're going to stick the glow sticks behind your ears so they light your antlers from the back. Then, we'll wrap each antler with one of these necklaces and stick them on with the mud."

Baxter huffed a great plume of steamy breath and bobbed her head in assent.

"Up close, it would look ridiculous. Someone would probably see you for exactly what you are. But, to an old man, in the dark, all the way down that walkway to the gate . . . You're going to look like a seriously bad dream."

"Perfect," she agreed. Martin finished pasting the glow-necklaces to her antlers with handfuls of dark mud.

They returned to within a few dozen yards of the gates, still deep in the shadows of the woods. "All right now," Baxter said. I'll take my place by the gate. You be ready to come and talk to him as soon as he comes out."

43

A thought suddenly occurred to Martin. "Oh my god, what if he sees you and shoots you?"

Baxter stood stock still. "I hadn't thought of that. I suppose I'm relying on his curiosity as a teller of scary stories to stay his trigger finger. Is he a hunter?"

"I don't know. I don't think so, but if a glowing, antlered beast was pawing at my gate, I might turn into a hunter real quick."

"Well, you stand back. You see anything that looks like a gun, you shout. I've got a trick or two might get me out in a hurry. I'm good at not being seen."

Martin nodded, silently.

Baxter approached the gates. She stepped a little to the left, then a little to the right, centering herself to the front door. She stood with her neck raised and her head pointed to the sky. Then she lowered her neck but raised her head a little. She took a few more steps, experimenting with poses, trying to find the best, most menacing angle. Once decided upon, she let out a series of low grunts.

Martin could hear them, but he doubted anyone in the house could. "Louder," he shout-whispered to her.

Baxter grunted louder, huffing and chuffing and pawing a little at the ground. She continued this way for a half a minute, but there was no response. She took a deep breath, raised up on her back legs, and came down hard on the paving stones.

There was a clatter and a light went on inside the house. Baxter continued to stomp and snort. Martin thought she looked like she was enjoying herself. Then she stepped her game up even more. She began raking her antlers back and forth against the bars of the wrought-iron gate. It made an awful racket. She huffed again. It sounded a bit like a bark and a cough rolled together. Her breath was making little clouds in the chilly Maine air.

The porch light clicked on and Baxter took a few steps back towards the shadows but continued to grunt and bark and shake her mud-coated, glowing rack.

"The hell is that?" Dale shouted from his front porch. "Who's making all that noise?"

Baxter kept up her show and Dale walked to the edge of the porch, right to the top step. She reared up again, came down, bucked, and stomped.

Martin saw Dale's mouth fall wide open. He didn't move for what seemed like a long time. Then, he turned to go back inside and Martin was sure he was grabbing a rifle. He gave Baxter a quick, panicked glance, but she didn't see it. She was too busy putting on her performance. She looked like she might be getting a little tired, though, and some of the mud was beginning to fall away as she continued her antics.

Dale came back outside, running right to the edge of the porch and raised a camera to his eye. "Damn," he said and took the four steps to the bottom where they met the flagstone walkway to get a little closer. He raised the camera again and muttered something else Martin couldn't make out.

Baxter was backing up to the edge of the wood and Dale was slowly walking down the path, trying to get a good shot with his camera. When he was halfway down the path, Baxter turned and bounded a few times into the overgrowth. Dale, his curiosity completely on the hook, dashed out through the gate and stopped, staring into the wood. Baxter hadn't gone too far. She wanted to keep his attention just a moment or two longer.

As Dale panned left and right, trying to spot the glow then catching it for a moment and losing it again, he wandered to just a dozen yards away from the gate.

Martin emerged from the shadows and brush. "Sir, I need to talk to you."

Chapter 9

Dale stood stock still with his hands clasped at his sides and his head slightly cocked. He remained that way for several seconds before finally saying, "Who are you and what in the nine hells is going on out here?" He continued to scan the woods.

"My name is Martin. That's Baxter. Come on out, Baxter."

Baxter trotted cautiously into the light. Martin stepped over to her and pulled glow sticks and rope off of her and showed them to Dale as if presenting evidence.

"Reindeer aren't native to Maine, son," Dale said as though that was the most pressing oddity before him. Perhaps it was the only element he could wrap his mind around.

Baxter was about to respond when Martin shot her an alarmed look. Baxter got the message. Maybe a *talking* reindeer would be a bit much.

Martin said, "She's come a long way. We need—I need to talk to you."

"Son, no one needs to talk to me," Dale put his hands on his hips.

"I do."

"Why?"

"Well, that's where it gets tricky. I have kind of a long story and a big problem. I think you'll want to hear one and you might be able to help with the other."

"I think you might have me mixed up with someone else. No one needs help from me. And as much as I love a good story, it's pretty late and you're a strange boy with a reindeer skulking around in the dark doing god knows what."

"Trying to get you to come out of the house," Martin said.

"What's that?"

"That's what we were doing out here. I know you're a horror writer, a fan of monsters and I thought we could draw you out of the house—"

"Why are you trying to draw me out of the house? Is there someone breaking in behind me? Do I need to go and arm myself?"

"No! We didn't . . . I didn't think you'd answer the door if I just knocked."

"You're darn right I wouldn't. You keep saying 'we.' You got someone else out here with you?" He looked over Martin's shoulder and continued to scan.

"Furthermore, I am not a writer."

"Sure you are. You might not have anything current on the shelves, but I've read your stories in Horrorpocolypse. I thought they were really good."

"You read those? Son, you weren't even alive when I wrote them. Hell, your parents were probably kids at the time."

"College age, actually."

"How did you come across those old things?"

"I was looking for them."

"Why?"

"I was researching you, sir."

Dale squinted a little and furrowed his brow.

"And what would you be researching me for?"

The truth would not earn him credibility. The author would probably think he was on drugs and pull the conversation's plug right then and there if he explained that a gingerbread man, one of Santa's elves, and a girl who essentially wielded the Christmas spirit had provided his name. "That's part of the story. A lot of it is probably going to sound completely insane. It sounds insane to me and I'm living it. I'm pretty sure you can help us, and I'm pretty sure we need you to."

"Where are your parents?" Dale asked, seeming to ignore everything Martin had just said.

"We're from Massachusetts. I . . . I tricked them into taking a trip here so I could find you. They're in a hotel in South Portland. I had to sneak out and I'm going to have to get back before they wake up."

"South Portland?" Dale asked, throwing his hands up in front of him in the "What the heck?" gesture.

"Yeah. Like I said, we've kind of come a long way." Martin nodded at Baxter. "She's pretty quick."

"Let me get this straight. You conned your parents into coming to Maine, snuck out of a hotel room presumably while they were sleeping, and rode a reindeer to my house where you pulled an elaborate prank to get me to come outside."

Martin stared at him, his eyebrows raised, fully aware of how completely deranged it sounded when strung together and said out loud like that. He shook his head.

"Maybe you'd better come inside. The reindeer is staying here, though."

Martin nodded again and said, "Thanks."

* * *

"So, like . . . There's something about you . . . your writing—maybe that . . . well it—"

"I'm not a writer."

"Okay. Maybe not now, but you were. You don't write anything anymore?"

"No," Dale said.

"Well, there's something about you . . . according to other fans," Martin made that up on the spot and kept going with it, "Other people who have read your stories and some people who say they know . . . they say there's a certain . . . spookiness to—"

"People say I'm spooky?" He grinned.

"Not exactly . . . but—"

"But, what exactly?"

Martin realized this was going to be harder to explain than he'd imagined, and he'd imagined it was going to be almost impossible. The only way forward he could see was straight through the crazy and right to the heart of the matter.

"Okay. Here goes . . . I was visited by Jack-o'-the-lantern. Apparently he's

. . . my great-uncle or something. He said there is this barrier, and there are worlds on the other side of it, like the underworld and stuff. They're becoming too powerful. They're gathering energy or something and . . . someone . . . actually the headless horseman, is going to use that energy to break through to our world.

"I went looking for help. I asked Sidney . . . the Peppermint Lightning girl . . . I don't know if you— Anyway, she did some research . . . her friends did. They found out that whatever makes this energy—they think it's fear-related, somehow—also . . . surrounds, or maybe comes from, your stories, from you. I don't know how or why and I'm not sure what good it does anyone, but I think, since you somehow seem connected to this energy, you can help stop the dead and the spirits and the demons and stuff from invading Earth." Martin took a breath and stared at Dale.

Dale pursed his lips, leaned back in his kitchen chair, clasped his hands across his not-inconsiderable belly, and cocked his head slightly. He stayed that way for what seemed to Martin a little longer than forever. Then Dale leaned forward again, put one forearm on the kitchen table and lifted his tea cup with the other hand.

"Now, that's crazy," he said.

Martin was about to reply when Dale cut him off. "It's a little too crazy for you to have made up and come all the way out here to tell me. So, I'm inclined to believe at least some of it is true or that you believe it is. But that doesn't change the fact that I have no idea what energy this is or how I'm supposed to help either."

This was not entirely true. Dale knew there was an energy. He'd felt it each time he wrote. He'd assumed it was passion for his work or the thrill of telling a new, terrifying tale—but maybe it wasn't that at all. He felt it every year when he began to write and, if he was being honest, he felt it whenever he thought about writing on the rare occasions he allowed himself to do so. He felt a little of it when he read other horror stories, and he certainly felt it on Halloween.

"This power, the energy, as you put it. You say it's too strong on the other side?"

"I think it needs to be balanced on both sides."

"And you think it's powered by fear?"

"I'm pretty sure, yes."

"So, to balance it, there needs to be more fear over here?"

"I guess," Martin said, shrugging his shoulders. "Maybe being frightened by things in our realm protects us against the other realm having the power to frighten us."

"I see." Dale took another sip of his tea and stood. He started to pace back and forth in front of the kitchen counter. It was clear he was thinking. Martin just couldn't be sure if he was considering how he could help, what he might know about the whole mess himself, or tossing Martin out of the house and slamming the door.

"The thing is, kid," Dale said, "I know you probably hope that you would show up here, I'd hear your story, and something would click into place. Maybe you thought I'd have an answer and you could go back to this spirit you've been talking to and set a plan in motion to save the world, but I don't. I don't have an answer."

Something had clicked a little, or at least came closer to clicking. This energy Martin mentioned—he couldn't stop thinking about it . . . even though what he wanted to think about was a practical way to help the kid and a good night's sleep.

Martin's chin sank a little closer to his chest. "That's okay. I knew it was a longshot."

"Now, don't sulk, kid. I didn't say I wouldn't try to help. I just don't have an answer."

Martin sat up straight. "You'll help?"

"Jeez, you go from sulky to giddy awful quick. You're apt to make an old man tired just talkin to ya. I'll help if I can think of a way. I haven't yet. But . . . Hell, I can't believe I'm doing this. I am definitely losing it. Listen, give me your phone number, or your email address, or both, I suppose. If I think of anything, I'll be in touch. But kid?"

"Yeah?"

"*I'll* contact *you*. You understand?"

Martin nodded.

"And I expect you'll keep anything between you and me a secret. I'm not looking to receive phone calls or interviews if strange sh— . . . stuff starts to go down."

"Top secret, Mr. Connors."

"Now, get back on your reindeer and go back to your parents. For crying out loud, I've said more ridiculous things talking to you tonight that I ever wrote for a horror magazine."

Martin giggled, rose, and shook Dale's hand. Dale reached into a kitchen drawer and produced a small spiral notepad and a pen.

Martin wrote his email address, phone number, and instant messenger handle. He didn't think Dale was likely to use the last one, but he'd have written his gamer tag too if it was another way the author could get in touch. He handed Dale back the notebook, thanked him again, and saw himself out the front door. He heard the lock click behind him and descended the stairs.

"So?" Baxter asked. She was scraping her flanks against the thick trunk of a pine tree. Clumps of drying mud lay in small piles all around her.

"Well, he didn't throw me out or call the police."

"That's good. What else?"

"He said he'd try to help if he could," Martin unwrapped the glow necklaces from around her antlers and stuffed them in his bag.

"That's not exactly what you were hoping for, I'd bet, but it's something."

"Yeah. It's *something*. You ready to go back?"

Baxter knelt down in front of him and he got on her back. She rose and took off at a run, Martin deep in thought with his arms wrapped tightly around her neck.

* * *

Dale sat back down at his kitchen table, tapping a rhythm on the polished pine surface with the pen Martin had used. It was hard to suppose the kid was lying. The story was too detailed, too specific, too insane. There was a possibility the kid was mental. The whole thing could be a delusion. He'd have been willing to accept this as the explanation for Martin's visit, if not for two things.

First, he'd arrived on a reindeer. Dale had seen the reindeer with his own eyes, and though they hadn't gotten back to exactly how he'd come to have a reindeer at his disposal, it leant a little credence to the story. Unless seriously unusual things were going on, people didn't just stumble across reindeer because it fit their delusion. The second thing was the business with the energy. He had to admit that he sort of knew what the boy had been referring too. He hadn't ever spent much time thinking about it before, but there was something to it.

Dale also thought about fear. It wasn't new territory for him. When he'd considered that he might one day be a writer, it was something he thought about all the time. He asked himself what was scary. He wondered over the nature of fear. He pondered ways to beat fear but more often ways to increase it, exploit people's nightmares to tell a great story. He began to consider the power of fear, the idea that it could be harnessed, could be wielded.

People wielded fear all the time. People used fear to control other people. Fear was the very best kind of political and social motivator. But that was a feeling, an abstract. What Martin had told him about was fear in a more literal way, a measurable quantity perhaps.

It was far too late, he decided, and the evening had been far too weird to plumb the depths of the nature and business of fear. He told himself he'd put a pin in that line of thinking until he was a little fresher. He needed to clear some mental desk space to dedicate specifically to Martin. It didn't feel entirely real, like he'd been drawn into an unusual live-action role playing game, but it wasn't a game at all, not if what Martin said was coming was actually coming.

Dale folded his arms across his chest and blew out a long breath. He had rules. He lived by a strict code when it came to his former ideas about writing. Taking up the pen had to wait. In a few days, it would be the end of Daylight Savings Time and he could take that one hour to work on his book. It occurred to him that he might work on it a little before that, by way of an experiment, a way to poke around with the energy, but he wasn't ready to allow himself to do that yet. Doing so would support Martin's idea that he was a writer, and he simply wasn't that. He couldn't, wouldn't be that.

Dale flipped the kitchen light switch to off and climbed the stairs towards his bedroom.

Chapter 10

Martin didn't know how long they had been gone, or how long the return trip had taken. He only knew if his parents had discovered he was gone, he was in serious trouble. When he'd climbed off Baxter, he thanked her and scratched her between the ears. He said, "Sorry. I can't stick around. I'd help you clean yourself off the rest of the way, but—"

"But you need to get back to your parents. Don't worry about it, sugah."

"Thanks, Baxter. It was kind of amazing to meet you."

"It was an absolute pleasure, Martin. Don't fret, though. You'll see me again."

"Christmas?"

"Possibly, but I was thinking sooner. I've already cleared it at headquarters to stick around a little while in case you need any more help."

Martin's eyes went wide.

Baxter smiled. "Go on. Get back to your room. I'm going to explore Maine tonight and I'll be back in your neck of the woods before you are. If you need me, I'll come to you."

"How will you—" Martin started to ask.

"Go," Baxter said and turned her rump towards him to punctuate the end of their conversation.

The elevator ride felt like it took forever and the hallway seemed way too long, but he finally arrived at their room. He paused to try and slow his breathing and the thumping in his chest. He listened at the door to see if he could hear either of his parents. It was silent. They were still asleep, or they weren't in there at all. He swiped the room key against this door's sensor and let himself in, holding the door as it closed to make sure there was minimal sound. He crept deeper into the room and heard a snore from his father.

"That's one," he thought. He checked for a light under the bathroom door. There wasn't one, and there were no lights on in the room. "That's two."

He blew out a heavy sigh and walked quietly the rest of the way to his bed. He peeled his clothes off and wriggled into his pajamas. Once he'd settled in under the covers and adjusted his pillow, he found he was giddy like Dale had said. He'd gotten to Maine, talked to Dale, and returned safely to his hotel room without waking his parents. He couldn't wait to tell Sidney.

He was playing over the future conversation in his head when it occurred to him he needed to tell Jack, too. He lifted his head from the pillow and looked around in the dark room, half expecting Jack to pop up from somewhere and want the story. When no apparitions appeared, he settled back down, closed his eyes and drifted off to sleep.

* * *

Rising early the next morning to frost on the hotel room windows and the sounds of a hard working heating system, Martin and his family decided to find themselves a big breakfast before finishing whatever Dad wanted to do at the convention and heading home. They found a mom & pop diner and ordered enough food to feed several more people than just the three of them. Bellies stuffed, they discussed the plan for the rest of the day.

Martin's dad said, "This has been outstanding. I can't believe you guys did this for me."

His wife smiled and pointed at Martin.

Dad continued. "I think I saw every booth yesterday, and I listened to a couple great panels. If there isn't anything you still want to do, Martin, what say we head on home? I was thinking maybe a hayride and picking pumpkins."

"Are you sure?" Mom asked.

Dad nodded.

"There're still more panels today, Dad. And we have the passes already."

"I know, but I don't think it could get any better. Now, I've had this big breakfast. The sun is shining. The air is crisp. It just feels like a good time to wrap it up and a great day for a pumpkin patch. You in?"

"I'm in," Martin said with a smile.

"I'm in," said Mom.

They paid their check and headed back to the car. None of them noticed the conspiracy of ravens perched in trees at the edges of the parking lot.

It was a lovely ride back along the New England coast. Dad was driving this time, so Mom could look out the window. As he drove, he told them both about things he'd seen at the convention, even though Mom had seen some and Martin had seen all of the same things. Martin was pleased that his father had enjoyed it so well. It made the guilt he felt over the ruse lessen significantly.

Mom commented on the leaves that still remained in the trees and the quality of the autumn light. Martin enjoyed the peace and, for a short time, the events of the past several days relaxed their grip on his mind. He had been planning on sending a message to Sidney telling her all about his visit to Dale and the way he and Baxter had gotten the author from the house, but decided it could wait until he was back home in his room.

He didn't want to be one of those kids who don't interact with their families because their faces are glued to their phones all the time. So, he sat and listened and talked with his parents a little about what he was working on in school, his pumpkin carving ideas—which were always elaborate though never quite panned out, and what he was thinking of dressing as for Halloween.

"I was thinking about doing some kind of ghost thing, but not just a sheet. If I go that way, I'm going to want to light it up from the inside and do something totally different."

"That would be interesting," his mother said.

"No superheroes, clowns, or ninjas for you then?" Dad said.

Martin gave his father a playful scowl. They'd had that conversation before. It was fine for little kids to dress up as Spider-Man or Batman or their favorite Teenage Mutant Ninja Turtle, but he felt strongly that Halloween costumes should honor Halloween: ghosts, witches, devils, monsters of any stripe. He supposed Freddy Kruger or Michael Myers were okay too, but wasn't into the bloody stuff. Frankenstein's monster, Dracula, the Wolfman, and the Mummy were okay, but not if they were too cartoony.

"You know our Buster is . . . particular about his costumes, hon," his mother said.

"I know," he said. "I was just pulling his leg. I have an idea for you, and I think it fits within acceptable parameters."

"We'll see. What is it?" Martin asked.

"The headless horseman."

Martin coughed and choked on the cider he'd been drinking.

"You okay?" his mother asked.

"Uh, yeah. Yeah, I'm fine. I just . . . er . . . swallowed wrong. The headless horseman? Where did you get that idea?"

"Oh, I don't know. You like it? I thought it was appropriately scary, authentic Halloween feel, and you don't see many of them," said Dad.

"Tricky without a horse though," his mother suggested.

Dad grinned, knowing the reaction he was going to get, "You could always get one of those inflatable costumes that looks like you're riding a horse."

Martin lowered and shook his head. "It might as well be a My Little Pony then, Dad."

"Stop," his mother said. "You two . . ." she left the rest of the sentence unspoken. "I do like the idea. What do you think, Martin?"

Martin was quiet a moment. He liked the idea. It could be a very cool costume. Under other circumstances he might run with the idea, but given his current situation, or possibly the situation of the entire mortal world, he wasn't sure it was in good taste.

He was not about to explain that to his parents, though. They were very protective of their only son. It was why he hadn't brought them in on Jack's mission. He knew if he told them, best-case scenario they'd assume he was having some Halloween fun, or worst-case scenario get his head examined. If he offered some kind of proof; an appearance by Jack, the talking cat Lilith, or Baxter, they wouldn't let him outside the house until they'd come up with their own solution and taken over the whole ordeal themselves.

"I like it. I'll have to think about it a little—see how I'd want to do the flaming pumpkin head."

"Without fire," his mother said.

"Of course. But without little LED candles either."

Martin's moment of peace had been broken. The drive was still pretty. His parents were in good spirits and it was a nice place to be, but the costume suggestion from his father had torn down any temporary reprieve he had from thinking about the coming invasion of the other worlds. He decided if Jack couldn't offer any more help, and he didn't hear anything from Dale for a few days, he had to tell his parents what was going on.

They wouldn't believe him. They wouldn't believe any of it was real, but he had to try because they had to be prepared if something terrible was going to happen. He had a growing sense—a heaviness in his gut and a pressure at his temples—that something terrible was indeed going to happen, and he hadn't been able to do anything productive to stop it.

* * *

Jack sat on the front step of Martin's house, right where Martin had been doing his homework when he'd first visited the boy. No one in the mortal world could have seen him sitting there because he wasn't using any energy to make it possible for them to do so. Cats could see him. They could see him just fine, he thought with chagrin as Lilith sauntered across the lawn and sat down beside him.

"They aren't back yet," she said.

"I can see that. Do you know what he was up to?"

"More or less. There's someone in Maine he thinks might be able to help. It isn't someone he knows, so he was going to try and get an audience and ask for help."

"Get an audience? Was it the bloomin' king, then?"

Lilith stretched and lay down in a sunny spot near where Jack's feet should be. "Of course not. I just enjoy the language more than you."

"So, who is this person and how is he supposed to help?"
"You'll have to wait for the boy."

II

Part Two

Chapter 11

"Something isn't right! Something is wrong. Something is not the way it is supposed to be or it is the way it's not supposed to be!" Gump said.

"What are you on about?" asked the raven.

"Something has happened. I was in my bed. I was sleeping. Maybe I wasn't sleeping because I noticed the thing I noticed, but I could have been asleep and noticing it woke me."

"Gump, you'd better take a deep breath and explain or I'm going to peck you in the snout." The plump little goblin resented the snout comment. He looked nothing like a pig, he thought, even if he had become a little more round since making his home in the mortal world.

"No," he said.

"No?" asked the raven who didn't have a name when he was with his conspiracy but who Gump had taken to calling Charlie for reasons beyond the bird's understanding or awareness.

"You know I don't like it when you say things like that to me. I don't like it at all."

"You have my sincerest apologies," Charlie said. "Now, please tell me what has you so upset." He flew ahead to a branch in the next tree down the lane Gump was walking. The sun had risen, but the mist was still heavy on the ground, and there wasn't much foot traffic in the park. It was chilly enough on mornings this time of year that the usual walkers and joggers were beginning to thin out.

"There's a thing that happens at Halloween. Well, it happens a little. It used to happen more. It used to happen when it wasn't just Halloween. It still happens when it isn't Halloween, just not as much and a lot less often, but almost never like it did."

"Gump. I know you're upset, but you are going to have to try and untangle that for me. I didn't understand a word of it."

Gump clenched his pudgy fists and scowled.

"Now, don't be upset with me. *You* came looking for *me*. I want to hear what you're trying to explain. It could be important. It's clearly important to you. But I don't understand what you're getting at."

Gump drew in a long breath through his snout-like nose and tried again. "On Halloween, there is a thing that happens. I don't know how to explain what it is. It happens sometimes when it isn't Halloween, but not as much. It used to happen a lot more often and a lot more powerfully when it did happen on Halloween than it does now."

Charlie thought he followed, so he bobbed his head. But it would be most helpful, he thought, if there was something more to it than "a thing happens." He was starting to get a picture, though.

"Okay. Continue," the raven coaxed.

"It happened last night. And it happened big, a lot bigger than it should have since Halloween is still a ways off."

"Is it a good thing, Gump? This thing that happens?"

Gump thought about that for a moment. "It's not a bad thing. It reminds me of my old home, though—on the other side. It reminds me of a long time ago." He said this not with nostalgia or homesickness, but quite matter-of-factly.

Charlie was on to it now. "I see. I think I know what you're referring to. I may have felt it, too, though if we're talking about the same thing then it certainly didn't strike me as profoundly as it struck you."

"I wasn't expecting it. I expect it when it's supposed to happen. I've gotten used to it mostly happening when it's supposed to. It scared me. I was scared that it happened in the middle of the night."

"I see that, my friend. I do. Do you think it happened near here?"

The question put a smile on Gump's face. It wasn't the reaction Charlie had been expecting. "Oh! It might have."

"Is that a good thing?"

"It might mean Halloween is coming early!"

"I'm sorry. Halloween isn't going to come early." Though true, Charlie found himself considering the growing strength of the outside realms, and that the rider might make his move early if he felt he'd amassed enough power. Halloween was the night the veil was thinnest, the time of the easiest crossing of spirits and other beings from beyond to this world, but if the rider had gathered enough power, it could happen any time.

Gump frowned.

An idea occurred to Charlie and he hopped up and down on a branch with much less dignity than was becoming a raven. "But it might!" he said.

Gump cocked his head and looked at the bird like the bird often looked at him. "What?"

"Not literally, I don't mean. Sorry. The celebration of Samhain, of All Hallow's Eve, is going to occur on October 31st like it always does. This is a date affixed to the occasion by man. The celebrating might come early, though. Gump, what first brought you here to this side?" He knew the story, but he wanted to hear the goblin articulate it.

"Well, it was Halloween. There was a lot of us. A lot of my family and a lot of other families. Spirits came. Goblins came. Devils came. I don't know what else. There was a lot of us. We came to explore. Something *called* us. People did, I think. They wanted us to be here, I think. So, we came."

"What attracted you to it, Gump? Did you come because the others came or was there something about it?"

"I think I came because they came—but then I stayed. It felt good on this side. There was something like it about home but very much not like home. And the treats!" Gump could feel his mouth start to water, and Charlie watched the goblin's eyes glaze over a little.

"The treats, Charlie!" he said. "I came that time and I saw the treats. I tasted them. There were cakes and sweet breads. There were baked apples and—"

"And you couldn't believe your eyes, your ears, or your nose. I know. I wasn't getting at that, though. We've gone off track."

"And I kept coming back," Gump continued. "Every year I came back, and sometimes I would stay until I could barely get back through. It was like I was getting pinched somewhere between the worlds. And then, not a very long time ago, I tried to squeeze back through and I couldn't get back at all. But the treats! Oh, there are so many more kinds now and you can get them anywhere! People just open up the trunks of their cars and they give out handfuls, Charlie! Have you seen it?"

"I have. There are a lot of treats."

"Not very many tricks, though." Charlie perked up at hearing this. "There used to be more tricks. I think that's why so many used to come. I think it's what made it easier to come. Something like that with the coming, anyway. Tricks and shrieks. Pranks and screams. Scares and giggles." This last was almost sing-songy.

"Gump, the feeling of those tricks, those things you say there are less of now, is that the thing that happened?"

"What thing that happened?" He looked genuinely confused.

"The thing that happened last night that usually happens on Halloween and so on?"

Gump's eyes went wide. "Yes! Has someone played a trick?"

"They very well may have. Someone may have played a great trick or come up with a keen prank. Someone might have had a good scare." Charlie had felt it. There had been a ripple in the air and then a crackle, then a jolt. Charlie had noticed but not paid it much mind.

As a creature of both sides, he was used to the movement of the energy and never paid much attention to where it came from. But for Gump to have felt it and connected it to both home and Halloweens of old, Charlie knew it had to have happened on the mortal side, on this side of the veil. Someone was calling the lightning.

Chapter 12

Beneath the front porch of the Kelly family home, Lilith was hunting. Martin had slipped her a can of tuna and a bowl of milk, so she wasn't hungry. This hunt was neither for feast nor fun. She darted into the dark corners, swatting and then darting again. Her prey skittered from her reach, weaved in and out of the porch's lattice work, and mostly evaded her jaws.

Spiders don't always deserve the reputation they have. More often than not, they are harmless. However, spiders are able to communicate with their kin through the veil and can be enticed to spy. Legends and folklore portray some spiders as helpful and others as devious and even malicious. Lilith recognized the spiders beneath the porch as children of Anansi—the trickster.

The rider had tired of waiting on the ravens who passed in and out of his domain to bring him news. They were willful and unreliable. But he had other means of checking up on Stingy Jack. It had taken almost no convincing. The greatest spiders of the realms on his side of the veil had no love for humans. Portrayed as objects of fear, crushed under foot, or swatted with whatever lethal object was at hand, spiders fell to humans by the score. Some of their more renowned ancestors were eager to balance the scales.

When the rider explained that his ambitions were soon to be realized, and promised Anansi a place of power and respect in the world he intended to create when the veil fell, the spider had agreed to call on his kin in the mortal world. These kin reported they had seen Jack-o'-the lantern, and gathered in greater numbers in the shadows and crevices of the Kelly home, waiting for him to return.

* * *

Sidney hadn't responded Sunday afternoon, and Martin didn't want to bother her again. She'd already been so much help, but he was eager to talk to her. He'd fallen asleep easily that night with no visit from Jack, much to his surprise. Unbeknownst to him, Lilith had harassed the spirit about letting the boy sleep and had then resorted to stalking around his house in the night to keep old Jack at bay.

Monday morning, while he stood on the frosted grass at the bus stop, Lilith sauntered up to him. "Good morning, Martin," she purred.

"Good morning," he said and reached down to scratch between her ears.

"Did you have a good trip?"

"I think so," Martin said. "I rode a reindeer. Her name is Baxter. She and I scared Mr. Connors out of his house. We spoke. I think he's going to help—if he can find a way."

"A reindeer? Interesting. Unexpected. I like it. It's good you spoke to Mr. Connors. I'm sure you were convincing. Jack has been pacing, waiting to hear from you. He tried to visit you last night, but I told him if he kept you up all night I'd scratch his eyes out."

"Oh. Thank you."

"No need. He'll want to visit tonight, though, I'm sure."

"I figured. I don't have a lot to tell him, though. I haven't saved the world yet or anything. Any news on your end?"

"My end?"

"I mean from the other side or—"

"No. I don't think so. I laid on the porch. I chased a bird. I did a little hunting." She was reluctant to tell Martin there were eyes on him, watching for Jack. Knowing would only unnerve him more than he already was. She kept it to herself. If later he needed to know, she would tell him.

"Okay," Martin said.

The bus came. Lilith strolled back along the driveway towards the front porch and Martin was off to school.

It promised to be a long day. Martin liked school well enough; he was a slightly above-average student in reading, an average student in science and social studies, and struggled a bit in math. He got along well with most of his classmates and his teacher well enough. He didn't love school, but he knew he didn't have to as long he was doing the work.

After the kind of weekend he'd had . . . Saturday night's adventures and a pleasant Sunday with his parents made Monday a little harder to face, and he knew his head wasn't going to be in the game at all.

He'd be asked to solve linear equations, but there wasn't likely to be room for the computation when much of the room in his brain was taken up by worrying if the world was really going to end.

* * *

Dale felt guilty he'd broken his own rule about writing. He wasn't an author like his young visitor had said. He was only a dabbler and only for an hour a year, and maybe a day in the coming leap year. He was uncomfortable in his own skin the morning after Martin had visited.

He'd been up at his desk, in the spartan little spare room where he kept his papers, his old attempts, and he had been writing. He wrote for an hour, maybe closer to two, and it had felt good, but it also felt wrong somehow. He reminded himself that he'd closed that door in his life and now was not the time to open it. He was too old. He'd moved on. He shouldn't have given in to the impulse.

But it *had* felt good. It had flowed from him. The energy of it—the power of the muse as he'd always considered it—was strong. He thought about that power differently the next morning. It felt like he was calling it out of the ether; and if Martin's story was to be believed, that's exactly what he was doing. But it wasn't the power of inspiration, it was the power of something else—something to do with his writing. What he didn't know for certain was whether it was a good thing or not. If he was in fact stirring up or attracting some power, was it something he should be doing? Given the explanation Martin had given him, he thought perhaps it was a good thing to have more of this power in his own world, but they were talking about forces beyond mortal understanding.

Though those forces were the focus of the manuscript he'd been working on and he considered them something of his specialty, his work was purely fiction. He didn't know the rules of it in the real world, assuming there were rules; assuming there was any truth to what Martin had said at all.

He stood in his kitchen that next morning, wrapped in a plaid terry-cloth robe, spreading blackberry preserves on an English muffin, waiting for the coffeemaker to finish its business, thinking about Martin. His thoughts had wandered back to his writing and the unease he felt about it, but the majority of his mental real estate was devoted to the young man. He thought a bit about Baxter as well, but there was at least a little less to consider there. She was a reindeer. She was in Maine. She'd been rolled in mud and decorated with glow sticks. Surreal as it all sounded, it was nothing compared to the conversation he'd had with the odd boy who'd apparently ridden that reindeer from South Portland to his house.

Dale set his English muffin down, rubbed his eyes with his thumb and forefinger and shook his head. What he found most remarkable about the entire experience was that he believed it. He found himself tending towards wonder that all Martin had described was real, and concern that if it was all real, they were in serious trouble. He wasn't ready to contact Martin just yet. First of all, he hadn't had his coffee, and a strong coffee could change his outlook entirely. Secondly, letting the boy know he believed him was a waste of time unless he could tell Martin he'd had an idea about what he might do about it all—what *they* might do about it all.

Chapter 13

"What I don't understand," Martin said, "is what you think I can do about it."

Jack spoke from the flame of the candy-corn-shaped candle his mother had on the dining room table. Martin would be in trouble if his mom came home and found the candle lit, or smelled that it, so he'd opened all the windows.

Lilith had met him on the porch steps when he came home off the bus and told him that he only need light a candle, and Jack would arrive. After getting him a snack, asking about his day, and checking to see if he had homework, Martin's mom had tasked him with "keeping the fort down" while she ran to the store.

No sooner had the car pulled out of the drive than Martin rummaged in a drawer in the china cabinet and pulled out the candle-lighting wand his mother used. He lit the little candle and stared at the flame. It danced, it sputtered a little, went still and danced some more. Martin had almost given up on anything happening when he heard Jack's voice.

"I thought maybe you'd forgotten about old Jack." Jack's voice was quiet, almost a whisper, though Jack didn't think he was whispering.

"Why the candle?"

"Easier than the pumpkin, isn't it?" Jack chuckled. "You can invite a spirit in with a candle. You probably didn't know that. Maybe that story has gotten lost, but if you know who you're looking for and they are looking for you, sometimes a candle can open a little gate to the other side."

"Are you back on the other side?"

"Thank the stars, no! I'm just conserving my energy and trying to keep my head down. I'm tethered to that side and I'm afraid the more energy I use on this one the more attention I'm apt to draw."

"Is that how it works?"

"I haven't a clue, to be honest. It might be. It sounds right. Better safe than sorry though, don't you think, lad?"

"I suppose."

After this preamble, Jack had asked for news. He wanted to know what had come of Martin's idea. In answer, Martin presented his question.

Jack answered, "What do I think you can do about it? I don't know. More than I can."

"That's it, though. You don't know if I *can* actually do anything."

"You must be able to. You're alive. You're on this side."

"But you were on the other side. Couldn't you do anything from over there?"

"Someone might be able to, but not old Jack. I'm not especially well-liked if you can believe that."

"If you're the same as a spirit the stories say you were as a man, I can."

"That stings, boyo."

"I'm sorry."

"That's my other question. Why do you want to keep the worlds separate? I mean, if we're going to be overrun by the underworld, and you're a part of that side, why aren't you rooting for that side?"

The flame sputtered a moment and Jack continued. "I don't believe I would benefit. I enjoyed life, you see. I don't know I knew that for certain when I lived, but it seems I did. I try to stay here as much as I can. I've escaped before and stayed until I hadn't the energy to stay any longer. My days on that side are dark, lad. And there have been so many of them."

"How do you run out of energy? What does that even mean?"

"I need the power to sustain me—to stay here. Not everyone does, not all the people and things from the other worlds, but the spirits and the things from lands of the dead. We need it to . . . stay together. Here, I can whip up a little scare, play a prank, haunt a bit and it's enough fright to top me off. That's gotten harder to do."

"I see," Martin said.

"Maybe you do. Maybe you don't. On this side, I also have freedom. There are rules that govern, of course. I can't walk around like a man. I have to tap into the energy to do much of anything other than watch and listen. On that side . . . well, you know the story, lad. You know what I do."

"Wander the darkness?"

"Yes. I carry my coal in my little turnip and I wander in the darkness."

"Then how did you escape?"

"Tricky bit of business that is, but I've managed." In truth, Jack had tricked another spirit he found in the wood into carrying a lantern like the one he was bound to. So long as there was someone lost in the darkness with the lantern, he could sneak away unnoticed, at least for a little while. Then, if he could slip through the gate like he had just a few days prior, he was free until he could muster no more energy or until the poor soul he'd fooled found his way out of the woods.

"Are ye going to tell me what you were up to on your little trip?" Jack asked.

"I made a trip to Maine. I went to see a man who writes scary stories. I'm told by a friend that an energy follows him; it's drawn to him or comes from him or something. Because it's scary stories he works with, I thought it might be the same energy."

The flame grew a little brighter. "It might be. I don't know," Jack answered.

"I don't know either. It's not like I can see it. I don't know if I can even feel it. I didn't feel anything the night I visited him, other than the fear of my parents discovering I'd snuck out of the hotel room."

"And is he going to help? Did anything come of it?"

"Not yet. Well, he had to think about it. He probably had to decide if he thought I was crazy before he even tried to think of a way to help. He's going to call me if anything occurs to him."

The flame dimmed again. "So, what now?"

"I don't know, Jack," Martin said, frustration coming through in his voice. "This isn't exactly something they teach in school. I'm fourteen and somehow I'm supposed to save the world from a coming invasion of the dead? I learned about all this like four days ago. I haven't had time to map out my save-the-world plan."

Jack was silent.

73

The flame didn't move for several long, silent seconds.

"Jack?" Martin asked.

"I'm here. Sorry, lad. I know it's all a bit much. Keep trying. Keep thinking about it. I'm doing the same. I'll visit soon."

Martin knew Jack was gone. He snuffed out the candle and fanned the smoke out the window as best he could. Then, he went to his room to have a very similar conversation with Sidney. He could only hope she had some ideas of her own.

Chapter 14

"I tried to help spread the Christmas spirit. What you've got to do is save the world from some kind of otherworldly apocalypse. Martin, I don't envy you at all. Worse, I don't know if there's anything I can do to help you."

"That's okay. I don't know if there's anyone who can. I mean, who has the expertise to deal with a thing like this?"

"No one I know. Oh, I can tell you that some friends of Emmett's did a little research on the Jack-o'-Lightning, though."

"The *what*?" Martin asked.

"Oh, that's what we've been calling it. You know, it's easier than calling it 'the power' or 'the energy' or something like that."

"Has a nice ring to it."

"I thought so. And it seems like maybe it works a little like Peppermint Lightning—although I guess we don't know if people can spread it the same way. But that brings me back to the research."

Martin was thrilled she had been talking to people about it since their last conversation. He hadn't expected it and knew how busy she was.

"Right," he said. "Thanks for—"

"No thanks needed. I couldn't sit by and watch this all fall on you. Besides, it was Emmett's friends, and Chester's too, who did the digging. It's sort of become an after-hours research project for them."

Martin had started the conversation sitting in his bed, legs crossed. Now he was up pacing the room. "What did they find?"

"Dale Connors is not unique. I mean, he seems to have an awful lot of this lightning, or is more charged with it or something, but there are others. Of course, all the letters in the archives are from children. These people would all be adults now, so it's hard to say if it's still with them."

"Okay. And there's no way to really know without meeting them."

"I don't think so. And you don't have time to track them all down and figure it out. It's not like there's some device you can measure it with."

"Someone from the other side might be able to tell."

"Possible, but you'd still have to travel. Jack would have to travel—or whatever it is ghosts do—to visit all these people."

"Won't work. I don't think he has the . . . power to do that. I don't know how much time we have, but I'm thinking Halloween is a likely deadline. Besides, I can't invent a bunch more trips all over the country. School. Parents. You know."

"Right."

"Yeah. Even with Baxter's help . . ."

"Right," Sidney said.

"So, we know that Dale isn't entirely unique. There are other people who seem to have some connection. We don't really know how that helps us, but it tells us . . ."

"I don't know," Sidney said. "Maybe it doesn't tell us anything, but it might come in handy. This is unknown territory."

"I hope Dale comes up with something," Martin said.

"Me too. Still haven't heard anything?"

"Not a word."

"Martin, if there was anything else I could do to help, I would. If I think of anything, or find out anything new, I'll reach out. But stay in touch, okay? Let me know what's going on, how you're doing, okay?"

"You got it," Martin said. "And thanks."

Martin ended the call, then tossed his phone on his bed. He had no idea where else to turn. He considered bringing his parents in on it, but decided against it, at least for the time being. He couldn't tell any adults at school about it because they'd think he was nuts, send him to the school counselor, then call his parents.

He thought about maybe telling some of his friends, but they would think he was nuts too. Even if they believed him, even if he could offer them proof, he didn't know what good it would do him.

He sat heavily back down on his bed and picked up his phone. He needed a distraction. He typed into the search engine, "headless horseman costumes," and began to scroll.

Chapter 15

The first advantage goblins have living in the mortal world is that, unlike the dead and some of the other creatures from beyond the veil, they don't have to feed on any kind of energy to remain. They can help generate some should they decide to play pranks or scare people, but they didn't need to. The second advantage they have is that they can pass for people as long as no one is looking too closely.

Gump was about three and a half feet tall, the size of a typical second- or third-grade boy. His feet were a little too large and his fingers a little too long to be inconspicuous, but if he wore regular shoes and tried not to gesture too much with his hands when he spoke, he could get by. A hat hid the pointy ears. He was a bit round about the middle—that had been increasing since he'd been on the mortal side of the veil—but it wasn't unusual for a child to have a few extra pounds either.

When he'd first arrived, he'd had a much harder time. After all, no shoes or hat, no human dress could hide his green skin. The green began to fade the longer he spent in the mortal world, especially if he stayed in the sun. Truthfully, it had more to do with eating the foods of the mortal world than it did the sun, but Gump was convinced otherwise.

His skin still held a bit of pigment that would stand out in a sea of more fair-toned people, but as long as he avoided wearing green he could get by. Every once in a while, someone would ask him if he felt well, but that was usually the worst it got if someone noticed there was something different about him.

Charlie had heard from some ravens he knew that there was something going on in a couple spots in New England. There'd been some kind of burst of energy somewhere in Maine, and the rumors had it that Stingy Jack was stirring something up on the other side of Massachusetts. Charlie had explained this to Gump the second time they talked about what Gump had felt the other night.

He decided they needed to investigate. After filling the goblin in on what he'd heard, Charlie said, "I'll tell you what, Gump; I'll fly out there and see what I can learn. I'll come right back. Are you going to be okay without me?"

"I'll come too. I can get to wherever you're going."

"If you walk, it could take you days. You'll have to stay off the interstate," Charlie said. "It wouldn't be safe and you're likely to get picked up by the police right away."

"I wasn't going to walk, Charlie."

"How were you going to get there then?"

"A bus."

"A bus? And where are you going to get bus fare?"

"Not sure. Are you certain you have to pay for busses? School busses are free. I've ridden them. I've ridden on them for not any money at all."

"Well, I know that. But you'd have to take a bus that goes across the state and they cost money. You'd have to buy a ticket."

"Do trains cost money, too?"

"Yes, Gump, they do."

"But I need to get around. A long time ago, I could have slipped out of this world then slipped back in somewhere else, but I can't get through any more."

"I know."

"I can't get through at all, not a little bit and not for a little while."

"I'm sorry, Gump. I wish I knew how to help you."

"You could fly. That's easy. I can't. That's hard."

"I'm sorry, friend. You might have to wait here for my return."

"What if you don't? What if I'm scared? Because I am, Charlie. Something is going on and something could happen to you or happen to me while you've flown away."

Charlie bobbed his head up and down, cocked it to one side in that uniquely bird way, and said, "I don't know what else we can do."

Gump scratched his head as he paced a little, looked to Charlie, and said, "Idea."

"No, I haven't got one."

"I've got one. I do"

Charlie cocked his head to the other side and said, "Do you? Let's hear it."

"I'm not sure you're going to like it. It's a little tricksy."

"Well, you tell me what it is and I'll decide if I like it or not."

Gump interlaced his fingers, scrunched up his brow and paced deliberately back and forth as he said, "A bus. I think the best way is a bus. I thought about hitchhiking, but that was dangerous. It is dangerous. I could get picked up by someone bad. I could get picked up and taken away, locked in a cage, stolen, kidnapped—"

Charlie interrupted, "Yes. Yes. Hitchhiking isn't a safe way to go. But, Gump, we talked about a bus and—"

This time Gump interrupted, "But we didn't talk about a tricksy bus. Well, the bus isn't tricksy, but getting on it is. Me getting on it. I don't think you could get on one and if you did get on one, I don't think anyone would let you stay."

"What is your trick for getting us on the bus?"

Gump ceased his pacing, scratched the top of his head—looking a little sheepish—and said, "You."

"I beg your pardon."

"You are the trick."

"You're going to need to explain that."

And he did.

* * *

A bus heading west across the state wasn't hard to find. They departed at regular intervals from the downtown terminal. The bus Charlie picked out was loaded well under capacity. He perched on the roof of the terminal and watched. Gump walked to the end of the short line of final boarders, doing his level best to look like he belonged there. As they'd agreed he should, Gump waited until the last person in front of him had taken a seat.

The goblin coughed.

Charlie took a breath and croaked, turning his head toward Gump. He hopped back and forth on the edge of the roof for several seconds, then swooped down and perched atop the bus's open door. The driver startled. He waved his arms at the bird, yelling, "Shoo!" Gump hopped up onto the bus, and then scrambled his way past the driver as if to get away from the bird.

Charlie spread his wings, beat them in the air a couple of times and let out a loud croak, looking directly in at the driver.

The passengers on the bus were leaning forward in their seats, watching and snapping pictures with their phones. The driver honked the horn. He shouted again. Then he pulled the lever to close the door.

Charlie took to the air, swooped in front of the bus, and alit on the roof. He leaned over and pecked at the top edge of the windshield for thirty seconds or so then—as quickly as he'd arrived—he was gone.

From the top of a telephone pole across the street, Charlie scanned the parking lot and, satisfied, took off to the west.

Gump made himself comfortable in a seat at roughly the middle of the bus and watched out the window as the bus backed up, then turned out into the street.

It was normally a two-hour trip, but with two or three additional stops to load and unload passengers. Charlie said it would likely take twice that. They weren't certain what their final destination was, but they knew it was to the west. Charlie would scout ahead and they'd rendezvous at the Springfield terminal. From there, they'd work out where to go next and how to get there.

Chapter 16

Martin left his phone in his backpack during school. It was policy and he did a good job of following the rules. It had been a lengthy, arduous negotiation with his parents to get a phone in the first place, and he wasn't about to get himself in trouble over it at school. That day he was having a hard time with it.

There could be a message from Sidney. She could have thought of something and reached out. Granted, she was in school, too, and probably had a similar policy, but she was a little older than he and things might be more lenient in high school.

There might also be a message from Dale. He didn't want to think too much about it because he didn't want to be disappointed if there wasn't, but the anxiety was building. There, in his backpack which he carried from class to class, was his phone which might contain a message about saving the world, and he couldn't look at it.

There was, in fact, a message. Martin wouldn't get it until he got off the bus. Bus drivers confiscated phones if they came out on the ride home. That wasn't official policy, and more than one parent had complained about it, but it wasn't worth the risk of losing his precious device. The message had been left shortly after lunch, about a quarter to one.

It said, "Martin, this is Dale Connors. I want to talk to you. Don't get too excited. I haven't found a way to save the world, but something has happened . . . that I think has some bearing on our situation."

When Martin played the message, his heart leapt to hear Dale's voice. It then crashed when Dale said, "Don't get too excited," then leapt again when

Dale said, "*our* situation." That meant Dale was in. He was considering this a real situation, and, furthermore, counting himself in on it. Even if he had no idea, it meant there was more than just himself and Sidney who were involved. He thought about Lilith and Jack and considered they were involved too, but they hadn't been so much a part of the solution as an observer and a plaintiff, respectively.

Martin could hardly wait to return Dale's call. He speed-walked into the house where his mother met him. "Hi, Buster. How was school?"

Martin loved his mother. He thought she was a top-shelf mom, but he didn't want to interact with her just then. Though if he didn't, it would be worse. She would worry something was off and pursue it.

"Pretty good," Martin said.

"Anything special happen today?"

"No. It was just another day. I did pretty well on that math test."

"What's pretty well?" Mom asked. She fixed him with a mock-menacing side-eye.

"It was a C—I think a C+ actually."

"That is pretty good."

"I know. It's not a B and it's not an A."

Martin's mom said, "But it's still respectable and I know how hard you have been working on it. Nice job."

"Thanks, Mom."

"The rest of your grades still looking good?"

"No change."

"Homework?"

"Nope. Well, a little. Mr. Daughtery wants me to correct the math problems I got wrong, but that won't take very long."

"Plans today?"

"No. I might go out for a bike ride."

"It's getting pretty chilly."

"I know, but it's only going to get colder, so I should get in my bike rides now." What he really meant was, "I need to get away from the house so you don't accidentally overhear anything that sounds completely insane when I call the author in Maine I snuck out to see while you were asleep."

"Fair point. Please wear a hat though."

"I can do that." Martin went to his room to change into a sweatshirt and pair of jeans. He grabbed a hat from the coat closet and bid his mother goodbye.

"I won't be gone long," he called as he walked out the door.

* * *

As soon as Martin had pedaled beyond their street, he fished his phone from his pocket and pressed the key that brought up his voice mail. He listened to the message again, hit the key to save it and pulled up caller ID. He found Dale's number. He thought the author might call from a private, blocked number and was relieved to see it wasn't the case.

The phone rang three times and with each ring, Martin's heart beat a little louder in his ears. On the fourth ring, he prepared to leave a message and had begun to compose it in his mind when Dale answered.

"Hello."

"Hi, Mr. Connors, this is Martin Kelly."

"Ah, yes."

"I just listened to your message."

"Yes. Well, right."

There was a silence that made Martin think the line went dead or that Dale had changed his mind about speaking to him. Then he heard the man take a deep breath and blow it out in a quick puff.

"Martin, I think I understand a little bit about that energy we talked about."

"You do?"

"Certainly not everything—definitely not how to balance the forces of light and dark and save the world—but a little."

"Okay."

Dale continued, "I haven't been a writer for a long time. That's just a fact. I have certain rules about writing. I wouldn't have done any the night you came to visit, but I was curious."

"You wrote another story?" Martin asked. His next question was going to be if he could read it, but Dale continued before he could get it out.

"No. It's not a story. It's a . . . never mind that. I wrote a little. We'll leave it at that. The important part is that when I wrote, I'm pretty sure I felt it."

"The Jack-o'-Lightning?"

"The what, now?"

"That's what my friend and I are calling it."

"It's a little cutesy for me, but that works. We have to call it something. So, I was writing and I felt it. The more I focused on the writing, the more involved I became in the . . . in the story, the more I could feel it. It was like static electricity building in the air. It was like . . . it was like the moments before a storm breaks. When I finished, it seemed to fade away, but it didn't abate entirely."

"Oh. Wow. So, do you still feel it?"

"I think I do. And, truthfully, I wrote a second time and I know I felt it again."

"Were you writing a scary story?"

"Always," Dale said.

"You think maybe that . . . summoned the lightning."

"That sounds very severe when you put it that way. A little too powerful for me."

"What, you don't want to be like the Thor of fear?"

"See, now *that* I like. I was a fan of Thor in the Marvel comics when I was a kid. Norse mythology is fascinating."

"Me too, on both things."

"To answer your question . . . I think I might. I mean, I think I might have summoned it. Maybe it was already out there and I gave it a place to go."

"You're a Jack-o'-Lightning rod?"

"I suppose, but I like the "Thor of Fear" a little better now that you've gone and given me that title."

Martin chuckled. "So now what?"

"Aye, there's the rub," Dale said. "I know, or at least I think, something I was doing was focusing that energy. I don't know what I can do with that, what it means, how it affects the things you told me about, but it's something."

"Okay. Okay, that's good. Um . . . So, maybe I talk to Jack about it? Maybe he's heard something?"

"What do you mean?" Dale asked.

"Well, if you called down the lightning here, then maybe something happened as a result on the other side."

"You're more an expert on this than I am."

"I might know a little more, but I'm not an expert. Are you going to keep writing?"

Martin heard Dale sigh again. "I don't know if I can, Martin. Like I said, I have rules. I learned this thing, and it's sort of proven to me that what you told me about is real. And what I've felt—well, that might help you understand it a little better, but I'm not a writer. I'll try. Don't know if I can keep doing it. If not, and unless there's something else I can do to help, that's the end of the line for me."

"You just wrote—twice! Doesn't that make you a writer?"

"Martin, you seem like a good kid and you have an awful lot to think about. If all this is real and really going to happen the way you describe, you have more on your plate than anyone your age has business dealing with. But, I'm a heck of a lot older than you and I'm not going to argue with you about this. I'm not a writer. Don't push it. Don't call me and ask me to reconsider. I'll do what I can, and I'll call you if I figure out some way I can help."

It was Martin's turn for a silent moment. After a long pause he said, "Okay, sir. I don't really understand but—"

"You don't need to understand."

"Okay. Well, thanks for sharing what you learned, I guess."

"You're welcome, Martin. Good luck."

"Thanks." Martin ended the call. He slid his phone back into his pocket and pulled his hat back on tight. He'd felt a flicker of hope, maybe more than a flicker, and he needed to hang on to it. Maybe Dale wasn't going to keep writing, but it sounded like he was on board to help however else he could.

Martin had a little hope, but he was no further than he had been—no closer to balancing the power on both sides of the veil.

He had nothing to report to Jack. He couldn't help but be a little mad at

Dale. He was glad the man had called, but then he said he wasn't going to do anything with what he knew. Writing made something happen, but he wasn't going to do it again? Martin kicked the kickstand of his bike up and pointed the front wheel back home.

As he pedaled, a raven flew overhead.

Chapter 17

There was an abandoned, collapsing barn on the outskirts of Carlisle, Massachusetts. Several generations past, it had been one of many barns that dotted that part of the landscape. It was overgrown and full of dancing shadows. It was a place that parents told their children not to go because it might come crashing down; a place that, based on the tattered remnants of comic books and discarded beer cans, children went anyway.

Martin Kelly could now add his name to the list of area youth who found their way inside to conduct secret business. He sat in the large, open main room of the barn in a puddle of sunlight made by a wide hole in the building's roof. He'd brought a flashlight and a candle from the drawerful his mother kept, but neither was lit. Martin had scanned the corners of the room with the flashlight to make sure he was alone, then found there were enough holes in the place to allow ample light.

But it was still a little spooky and that was, of course, why Jack had chosen the location. "It will give the boy just enough unease that I can use that power to make myself seen," he said to Lilith. And he was there, sitting across from Martin with the cat persistently trying to make its way onto his lap. They had begun to discuss what little Martin had learned when a flapping of wings and an echoing croak burst through the hole in the roof. A raven the size of a rooster, Martin thought, alit on one of the few straight beams that once supported the barn.

"Oh, for the love of Set," Lilith said.

Martin scrunched up his brow and looked at Jack, who just smiled.

Charlie broke the silence. "Jack, I thought I'd find you here. Lilith," he added.

"Were you looking for me, raven?"

"In a manner of speaking. I'd heard you'd found your way back to this side and I was following a trail left from the other side."

Jack scratched his chin. He knew there was a good chance he was leaving a trail, but didn't know who or what would be able to follow. Now, he knew he could put ravens on the list next to cats.

"I hope I didn't startle you, young man. I am . . . well I don't usually use a name to be honest. Ravens just know one another, but a friend of mine calls me Charlie, so I suppose that's who I can be to you as well."

"I'm Martin," said Martin. "It's good to meet you."

"And the fact that I didn't terrify you or shock you when I spoke just now tells me that our meeting isn't entirely unexpected or peculiar to you."

"Well, I wasn't expecting more of us, but I guess I'm not shocked. Given my last few days, I think it would take a lot more to shock me than it used to."

Charlie cawed in what Martin deduced was the raven version of a laugh. It was not an entirely pleasant or joyful noise.

"What are you doing here?" Lilith hissed.

"I'm following a trail, feline. What are *you* doing here?"

"I'm helping save the world."

Jack laughed. "You are not! You're harassing a spirit and tagging along where you aren't wanted."

"Saving the world?" Charlie asked.

Martin replied, "Maybe. Something like that, anyway. I guess since you're here we'll fill you in."

"I'd be much obliged, but my friend is right behind me and it would be a favor if you'd wait for him. I'm sure he'll be interested as well."

"Why would we do you a favor?" Lilith asked.

Charlie ignored the question.

"Another raven?" Martin asked, afraid that if Lilith became outnumbered things could get truly unpleasant.

"No, actually. He's a goblin. He goes by Gump. He's been stuck on this side for years, got a little too used to humans and a little too fond of sweets to tell the truth."

"Why is a goblin friends with you?" Lilith asked.

"Hey, what gives here?" Martin asked Lilith. "What's the deal with you and ravens?"

Charlie hopped down from the beam and stood a few feet from Martin, cocking his head at the cat.

"Here we go," said Jack. He leaned back against a post and stretched his legs out in front of him.

"The cat was a revered go-between for many cultures around the world, known to all as travelers and messengers between worlds. Temples were built in our honor in the most ancient civilizations. We were kept in palaces all over Europe and parts of Asia, tasked with keeping malicious spirits away. We keep other spirits company. Sometimes we guide them where they need to go or show them the corners of the other world. Some people consider us guardians."

Martin looked at Jack, "She's your guardian?"

Lilith answered. "Your great-uncle Jack and I have known one another for some time. He knew my mother and her mother and so on. You see, when first cursed to wander the dark places on the other side, it was a cat who kept Jack from wandering too far."

"Bah!" Jack said and spat.

"But," Charlie interrupted. "They weren't the only kind known to travel. Ravens cross between worlds. From the Celtic druids to the Norse and—"

"You were the benefactors of irrational belief. People thought you good luck. Superstitions arose about cats, black cats in particular. Bad luck, people began to say. Steal the breath from babies, people said. We protected the innocent from evil influence!" She was pacing now, no longer interested in Jack's lap. Her ears, almost flat back against her head, twitched as she went on.

"The lore changed. Cats were seen as mouse catchers and house pets, and we lost our reputation. And then *he* betrayed us," Lilith said.

"Who?" Martin asked.

"The story teller. The poet."

"Not this again," said Jack.

"This!" Lilith said. "He had a cat. He had a black cat, and we spent many long days and dark nights together. I sat on his lap when he wrote his tales and by the fire when he was inventing them. He wrote poems about us. But those poems never reached the fame that *other one* reached."

Charlie flapped his wings and cried a single word, "Nevermore!"

Jack laughed. Martin's eyes went wide and Lilith spat again.

"That poem elevated the place of ravens, the poet forsaking the feline. Ravens are now a part of Halloween decor."

"So are black cats," Martin said.

"Yes, but we have moved aside. We are no longer revered. We are merely decorations."

"Aren't *they*?" Martin asked, nodding towards Charlie.

They might have been, but a conspiracy of ravens strikes fear. That dreadful film saw to that. Birds! No one was afraid of birds before. They have no mystery, no beguiling grace."

"What about humility?" Charlie asked.

Lilith hissed at him

"Wait. Afraid of birds . . . Charlie, do you scare people?" Martin asked.

"What? Intentionally? There are those who are nervous around birds the size of me and my kin, but I've never set out to strike fear, if that's what you mean?"

"Could you?" Martin asked.

"I see where you're going, " Jack said.

A figure that looked like a plump grade-school student crept between the slats Martin had entered and walked right up to their little circle.

"I'm Gump," he said, plopping down on his ample backside and taking a bite too large for his mouth from a Snickers bar. He had the courtesy to nearly finish chewing the bite before adding. "Charlie is my friend. I'm a friend of Charlie's. I followed him here when he flew. He found where to go and I followed right along."

"Good to meet you, Gump," Jack said.

"Nice to meet you," added Martin.

Lilith sniffed around him and meowed softly but said nothing. His ears were still tending towards flat.

"Gump," Charlie said, "Martin here was just asking me if people were afraid of me."

"I'm not," Gump said. "You're nice."

Charlie bobbed his head and said, "Thank you. I don't think that's what the young man was asking, though."

Jack stepped in, "Could you make someone afraid?

"I believe so," Charlie nodded.

"A lot of you could—like a cloud. A flock? What do you call it? A swarm?"

"A conspiracy," Charlie corrected.

"Okay, so a whole conspiracy could whip up a bit of fear."

"Likely," Charlie said. "Why is that important?"

Martin stood. He paced a few steps in either direction, biting his lip. He turned to Charlie and asked, "Have you ever flown as a conspiracy and felt people's fear or some other kind of . . . change?"

Charlie knew exactly what he was talking about. It was energy of the same kind that had led him and Gump to the barn. He bobbed his head up and down.

"We're calling it Jack-o'-Lightning," Jack smiled.

"Your idea?" Charlie asked.

"No, surprisingly."

Gump sat, shifting his eyes from one speaker to another, saying nothing but keeping up with the conversation nicely.

"So, you were discussing saving the world and this Jack-o'-Lightning has something to do with it? Given the abundance of it crackling around the other side, that certainly makes sense."

"Right," said Jack.

"Well, perhaps you should fill Gump and me in on the details, if you don't mind."

Martin was thrilled to have more interested parties. He was pleased enough that it didn't bother him at all that his new allies were a raven and a goblin. He half expected Baxter to waltz into the barn. Martin looked at Jack, expecting him to tell the story, but when Jack said nothing, Martin began.

"So, Jack came to me through a plastic candle," he said.

* * *

Martin had to stop several times in his telling of the tale to clarify, ask Jack to chime in, or answer questions. The story itself sounded no saner to him this time through than it had any of the previous times. That said, it did help his comfort with it that he was now also telling a raven and a goblin. Somehow their appearance had made it all *less* weird. By the time he was finished, everyone seemed pretty clear on the events so far on both sides of the veil.

Lilith hadn't participated much in the conversation and Martin wasn't sure if it was because she really was just along for the ride or if she was still being salty at the appearance of Charlie.

She sauntered into the middle of their circle just as Martin wrapped up with, ". . . and that's where we are."

She said, "Whether you care about the headless horseman's plot to tear through the barrier and overrun this world or not, you have to be concerned about the balance. Neither side should control, or be able to feed on, significantly more power than the other. Jack here has his reasons for wanting to protect this side of the veil, whatever you may think of them. Martin certainly wants to keep this side from being conquered. Gump, I'm not sure where you stand. I would think since you're on this side you would want to see it remain, but your family is beyond."

Before she got to him, Charlie chimed in, "I, too, am for balance. We live in both worlds. We answer to no lords."

"You have no allegiances," Lilith said quietly.

"No. We do not, and we view that as an asset. I have no love for the rider, nor do I have a stake here in this world. But Lilith has presented the core of the matter."

Jack stood and floated around the room. He was only visible from the calves up so he might have been walking, but Martin couldn't see it. The phantom had faded a little since he'd first arrived.

"Fine. Fine. Yes. Balance. Right now there isn't any and the more the scales tilt the greater the risk. I think we all understand that. That isn't the question. The question is, How? What do we do?"

Martin mentioned Dale again, but reluctantly since the man had said he wasn't going to write again, and so far that seemed the only thing that connected him to the lightning. Charlie had agreed that great black clouds of ravens would likely create the forces of fear they believed they needed to muster, but the raven wasn't sure he could convince his kin to do such a thing. As he'd explained, they had no stake in the coming battle. It would take convincing.

Lilith asked the question, "Have you ever seen a parade of black cats, a couple dozen, descend on a house or even a small town?" That had left them all with the impression she knew she would be able to help and she and her kin would be eager to do anything that stirred the powers. They might even be motivated by outdoing the ravens, or at least getting some of their esteem back—assuming that terrifying people would do that.

"We need the other side," Gump said.

"What?" Charlie asked.

"Ravens and cats and writers and kids are fine. Maybe bats and spiders would help, too. I get scared by them, but I don't know any to ask and I don't think any of us speak spider. Well, you might, Charlie, but don't tell me because I don't want to know what they would say."

"Not spiders," Lilith said. "The rider had already gotten to them."

Before she could be asked to explain, Jack said, "The other side?"

"Well, what if we had help there? What if there were people, things, others on that side that wanted to try to stop the rider? What if we could get them on our side? Maybe if they saw, if they understood balance, which I don't think they do, but they might because there are lots of different things on the other side, and some of them very smart, who understand a lot of different things. But maybe if they could see that there are people and things on this side that generate the Jack-o'-Lightning maybe they wouldn't want to try to tear it apart. I don't know how to explain it. I don't understand exactly how it all works but I think when you have two sides and one side is much smaller, maybe weaker, and I don't mean to call any of you weak, but there are only a few of us . . . I mean, if one side is much smaller it seems there are only two things you can do. You can make the small side bigger or the big side smaller."

Charlie cawed and Jack slapped his thigh. "Well said, young man!" Charlie said. "Now, how do we do that?"

"We need a quest!" Gump declared.

Chapter 18

At first, the strange council gathered in that decrepit barn had chuckled at Gump's insistence on a quest. Then, they realized he wasn't kidding since he sat stoically, which was not a typical aspect for a goblin. Charlie had been the first to notice, and pointed out that Gump was, in fact, serious. He explained what he meant by "a quest," but had a difficult time articulating exactly the kind of thing he had in mind. Charlie helped pull it out of him and translate where needed.

There had been much talk amongst the goblins—before the last time Gump crossed over—that the rider had been gathering objects from the mortal world and secreting them away in his realm. The goblins didn't know what the objects were or their value to the horseman. They only knew that when a curious party of them had sought one out and uncovered its hiding place, fear repelled them.

Gump had a theory. He believed they needed to acquire, or at least investigate, these objects. "If these treasures are from this side and he wants them on that side, we probably want them back on this side again. Some of the things that follow him may see those of us over here are clever and brave and that the rider can be tricked," he said.

Lilith said, "If we found one of particular value, one humming with Jack-o'-Lightning, all the better."

"Gump, did the goblins ever say exactly what these objects were or how many of them they knew about?"

"Never said. Maybe said, but not to me. Not very many, I think. Hard to get. Hard to bring back."

What they had the most difficulty with, beyond whether such a plan might in fact shift the balance, or whether the spirits of the underworld cared who controlled such relics, was how they would get there, find such a thing, and return.

"If I go back, I don't figure I'll be able to return," Jack said.

"And I can't," Gump said.

Lilith offered her abilities as a spy and scout but pointed out that if she found anything larger than a rat, she wouldn't be able to carry it back, and if the artifact was fragile, it could get damaged. Charlie's concern was much the same. He added that once on the other side, there were eyes on the ravens. The headless rider had approached them looking for information on Jack—a fact Jack had expected but was nonetheless unhappy to hear.

"That's two of us ruled out and a possible pair of scouts," Charlie said.

Martin replied, "I think we all knew where this was going from the start." He sighed and threw his hands up. "Sure! Send the fourteen-year-old to the world of the undead, and monsters, and demons, and everything else. What could go wrong?"

No one had an answer for him. They averted their eyes. Gump cleared his throat. Charlie preened.

Martin went on, "And there is the small matter of getting there. None of you have once mentioned a living person from this side travelling to that side."

"It's happened!" Jack said. "It used to happen that people travelled to the other worlds a lot. It's dwindled some. And I'll admit it's harder . . . and more dangerous. And I can't think of a time recently where I've heard about it . . ."

Charlie said, "Odysseus!"

"Not recent," Lilith replied.

"None of you are helping," Martin told them. "It doesn't matter if it has happened before. What matters is if I can do it, how I would do it, how I would keep from getting lost, eaten, tortured, killed, or worse."

Lilith strode toward him, nuzzled against his legs, and tried to climb in his lap. He was too agitated to be able to offer her a comfortable spot, so she settled for stretching out along his thigh as he sat cross-legged on the barn's bare earth floor.

They sat in silence, each considering the larger plan, how they might play their role, and Martin's plight. They all knew he was the only one of them who could find the rider's treasures and bring one back. Unless they could find someone on the other side who could bring one to them—and none of them knew anyone who might—they were out of ideas.

Jack broke the silence. "I can get you there."

Martin raised his head to look Jack in his empty, ghostly eyes. He was suspicious, but curiosity won out. "How?"

"My lantern."

Gump looked puzzled. "Lantern?"

"It can get him across the veil. It's how I first got from this side to that. The devil placed a coal in my lantern and forced me to roam the wood, only the path I took led me across to the other side where I continued to wander until I'd worked out where I was and the rules of the place."

"Assuming the lantern works for me, assuming I can then find some kind of holy artifact of fear or whatever it is the horseman is hiding, how do I know I can get back?"

Jack said, "The lantern is a thing of both worlds—both sides of the veil—as I understand it. I think it's how they know when I've escaped, incidentally. As long as I have it, I can cross back and forth. We have no reason to believe it wouldn't work the same for you."

"You have the lantern now?" Martin said.

Jack raised one of his ghostly arms and in his hand materialized the shape of a hollowed out turnip on the end of a short length of rope, a faint glow emanating from inside. "Always," he said. "I'm bound to it."

Martin said, "How do I carry a ghost lantern?"

Jack flickered a moment and said, "It isn't always a 'ghost lantern.' Leave that to me."

"It isn't looking very strong," Lilith said.

"Maybe it needs charged," Gump said.

"It will keep a path before ye in the darkness. It isn't much of one, never was for me, leastways."

"But I don't know where I'm going."

Charlie said, "We're going to try to take care of that for you." Lilith nodded.

Gump scratched his chin. Then he scratched his head. He wrapped up by wringing his hands together and said, "I can't help on that side. I can't get to that side. I want to help. I'll have to help here."

Jack nodded to him and Charlie said, "I'm sure you'll find a way. It's your favorite time of year and I am confident you will find some inspiration in that."

Gump nodded this time. Martin was worried, perhaps terrified. He thought if this was the kind of fear that attracted the lightning, he'd be crackling with it as he sat here in the barn. For all he knew, he was. There could be a great Jack-o'-Lightning thunderhead right over him and he wouldn't know because he couldn't see it, and he couldn't feel anything beyond his own fear of crossing the veil and what he'd find on the other side.

"Boyo, you should know the same laws don't apply on that side," Jack told said.

And Charlie clarified by saying, "He doesn't mean laws of the land. What you might call the laws of nature shift a bit from one realm to the next, though, as they've been gathered under one rule that is changing now, too."

Martin couldn't decide if he was glad they'd warned him or if this just made it all a little more awful. He decided it was both.

"I'm going to try to act normally, you know? Go to school, do my homework, talk to my friends, play video games, and be a fourteen-year-old while you check in with the ravens and see if they have any idea where I'm supposed to find what I'll be looking for," Martin said to Charlie. "The rest of you . . . I don't know. Lilith, what do you think about keeping Gump company and maybe helping him brainstorm?"

Gump said, "Charlie told me cats are pompous and self-righteous, but you seem nice. That would be fine." Lilith fixed Charlie with an icy stare and gave him an abbreviated howl. Charlie did that thing that might have been laughter and took wing.

"I'll be back," he said.

Jack stood. "I suppose I need to work out the lantern?"

"I'd say so," Martin replied.

"I 'ave an idea. It's a risk—to me—but if this plan of ours doesn't work and we don't come up with another, I'm done for no matter what."

"No pressure," Martin said, shaking his head. "Later, Jack."

"Ta," Jack said and faded from sight.

"I'd better get home. Good luck you guys," Martin said to Gump. "I guess I'll see you when Charlie gets back, unless something happens in the meantime. Good luck."

"Good luck to you, Martin," Gump said and Lilith repeated the same.

Martin squeezed out through the broken slats in the barn, pulled his bike from where he'd hidden it in the brush, mounted, and said to himself, "How in the world . . .?" and pedaled home.

* * *

Martin messaged Sidney as soon as he'd reached the safety of his room. *I hate to bother you, but I need to tell someone what the plan is, if you can call it that, and I can't tell my friends or my parents.*

No bother at all. You okay?

I'm not really sure. Right now, I'm just waiting for information, but that information is going to get things going. And things are scary.

Martin described the meeting in the barn in as much detail as he could.

Is Baxter still around? Sidney asked.

Yeah. Unless there's another reindeer in Carlisle, I spotted her in the woods yesterday. Why?

I don't know. I was just trying to come up with anyone who can help. I don't know what she could do for you right now, but I'm glad she's there.

Martin said, *Me too. She would have fit in nicely in the barn between the talking cat and the talking raven . . . or maybe between the ghost and the goblin. lol.*

Trust me. I know exactly what you mean.

Do you think any of your other friends could help?

Well, Emmet's no good with fear, but he might have friends who can think of something. Chester . . . a cookie in the underworld . . . That sounds like a cool movie, maybe. I don't know. I'll ask.

Is it something you could approach . . . the big guy over?

I thought about that. Maybe. I mean, we are talking about the end of the world as we know it and that would certainly put a kink in Christmas. I'll ask the guys when I talk to them.

By "the guys" Martin assumed she meant the elf and the gingerbread man.

Martin, if you don't fix this, all my work goes up in smoke. Sidney added a smiley emoji at the end of the sentence, and it did make Martin smile a little, but it also added some weight to the rock already sitting in his stomach.

The end of the world does probably mean a lack of Peppermint Lightning. I don't know, maybe the hordes of the dead will want to celebrate the holiday season festively, too. Let me know what you find out. Meanwhile, I have to go eat with the folks.

Sorry you have to carry this, Martin. You're brave for even considering it.

Thanks. I just hope I can go through with it. I'm not feeling like I have a lot of choice. Talk later.

Later.

Martin put his phone back in his pocket and went downstairs. He wanted to have a perfectly normal dinner with his almost perfectly normal parents and think about perfectly normal fourteen-year-old things for a little while.

Chapter 19

Waiting around to find out where in the underworld you need to go to save the world while behaving like a perfectly normal eighth grader is no easy feat. Doing so without alerting your parents to the fact something is going on is even harder.

After the first two days, Martin's mother and father, who had already sensed something unusual in Martin's behavior, had a conversation about what could be out of the ordinary with their son. After another two days, Martin—at this point worrying if something had gone wrong with Charlie, if perhaps he'd been caught scouting by someone or something that didn't appreciate it or if he'd somehow become trapped on the other side—was becoming visibly agitated, at least to his parents.

On the fifth day from the meeting in the barn, Martin was sitting on the steps of the front porch of their home, his chin in his palms and elbows on his knees. He'd been checking in with Lilith each day to see if she'd heard anything. There was nothing from Jack. She hadn't lost his trail, though. She'd slipped in on him a couple of times—hiding out in a local watering hole after hours, as usual—to see what progress he was making with the lantern situation. He hadn't shared any news, good or otherwise.

Gump was busy cooking up some tricks, she'd told him. The goblin had made the barn his personal base of operations. Most alarmingly, there was nothing from Charlie. Martin had also been holding out hope that Dale would come around, that maybe he'd decide to write more after all, since the fate of the world seemed to rely on shifting the very power he stirred up when he did. Dale hadn't reached out either. Sidney was busy. They had exchanged only a pair of brief messages.

Evidently, she'd contacted her friends in the north, but as yet they were unable to come up with ways that they might help. Martin wasn't surprised. After all, they were the creatures of Christmas and fear was not their stock in trade. So, Martin sat on the porch alone, feeling very much adrift, when his parents came outside.

"Buster, it's getting awfully chilly out there," his mother said. "Why don't you come inside?"

"I'm okay," Martin said.

"Come on, son. What are you doing out here anyway?"

"Nothing. Just . . . I don't know. Chilling."

His father put his hand on Martin's shoulder. "Listen, your mother and I want to talk to you and I know we don't really want to sit here in the cold. Would you come in, please?"

"What do you want to talk about?" Martin asked.

"We want to talk about why you're sitting out here, alone on the porch in the cold and dark."

Martin sighed. He hadn't realized how dark it had gotten. It was late enough in the month the sun was going down when they ate supper. He realized it was pitch dark then and had been for a little while. Martin had turned the plastic pumpkins around and switched on their LED lights, otherwise there was only the glow coming from inside the dining room window and a sliver of a moon.

"Okay," Martin stood and the three of them went back inside.

His mother had put some cookies on a plate in the middle of the dining room table. She had wanted to put hot chocolate out as well, but her husband said it was too much. It would be too obvious they were trying to soften him up before asking him the questions they wanted to ask.

They didn't have any experience with this sort of thing. Martin wasn't the kind of boy who had to be sat down to have a family meeting. He'd gotten in a little trouble now and then, but it was the kind of trouble you just came out and addressed at the time. One of them would accuse. Martin would plead guilty. Grounding or a sentence of no PlayStation would be handed down and it was over. This was new ground, and both of Martin's parents worried that it was only the beginning since Martin was a teenager and showing signs of strange behavior.

"You aren't in trouble, Buster," his father said. "We're just a little concerned about you lately."

Martin looked his dad in the eye for a moment and could see the concern there, accompanied with a slightly furrowed brow.

"You've been acting a little strange lately," his mother added.

Dad turned to her, "I thought we decided against 'strange.'" Then he turned to Martin, "Different. Unusual. Out of sorts, maybe."

His mom nodded and Dad continued. "You know if there is ever something going that upsets you, you can come to us, right?"

Martin nodded.

"And you won't be in trouble if you need to tell us something that's bothering you. Sometimes you just need to get it out," Mom said.

Martin nodded again.

Dad had hoped that would get his son talking, but it hadn't. So he pressed on. "It doesn't matter if it's about school, or girls, or if someone has approached you about drugs. We want to help."

"You can trust us," Mom said.

Martin gave them a toothless smile and nodded again, "I know," he said.

He knew he was on the hook. There was no denying that something was wrong. His parents sensed it and had arranged this dining room table intervention to address it. He'd told himself if they asked him directly he wasn't going to lie, so in his silence he had been trying to come up with as vague a way as possible to tell them the truth.

"Martin," his mom said, "is there anything you want to talk about?"

Martin took a deep breath and said, "A friend of mine is having some trouble. He asked me to help and I've gone to a few other friends. We've been talking about it but haven't come up with a way to help yet. I'm just worried about him and the trouble he told us about." There, Martin thought. Nice and vague and entirely true.

Dad had that furrowed brow again. "What kind of trouble is this friend having?"

Uh-oh, Martin thought. He hadn't been prepared for that. "He . . . uh. It's kind of about a bully."

"Kind of?" His mom asked. "Which friend is this?"

Martin's heart was pumping faster now, and he could feel his palms beginning to moisten. In his head, he was pleading for them to ask no more questions, to get no more specific with them if they did. He was barely treading water as it was. He thought at this point they were going to be able to see him sweat and then they would know he was holding something back, or worse, lying, and then he'd have to spill it.

"Well, this guy . . . he's not really bullying my friend directly. . . Jack—my friend Jack—this bully is really threatening a whole bunch of people."

"Who's Jack?" Mom asked. She knew all his friends and there were no Jacks among them.

"And how is this other boy threatening them?

"Jack has been around a while. I just haven't . . . I never mentioned him before because I didn't really know him, but we've been hanging out."

"And this bully? Who's he and what kind of threatening are we talking about?" Dad asked.

Martin was having a meltdown, internally. He couldn't keep up with his own thoughts. His hands were really sweaty. He didn't dare reach for a cookie, and Mom would find that suspicious on its own. Dad was zeroing in and he was losing the thread of his own story. Martin was pleased with himself that he'd gotten this far without any falsehoods, but it was getting tricky.

"The other guy—he's from New York, upstate—he um . . . he's threatening to take over."

"Take over what?" Mom asked.

"The whole place," Martin said with a quaver in his voice only his parents could have put up with.

Dad said, "Let me make sure I have this right: There's a new kid at school, a bully. He's threatening to take over. What, the school? The town? And you and some other friends are trying to come up with a way to help your new friend Jack?"

The jig was up. If he said no, then his parents would be upset he wasn't being forthright with them. If he said yes, he was lying to them. But telling them everything . . . the whole truth? He was risking sounding insane. He was risking them trying to stop him. They were concerned enough and maybe suspicious enough, and his story sounded crazy enough that they'd probably decide he was being evasive and dishonest and the heat in the room would go up.

"Sort of," he said.

* * *

Mom had already been sitting. She was in the chair across from him instead of at one end of the rectangular table. Dad had been standing, but now sat in his chair at the end nearest the kitchen. "Okay, Buster." he said, looking Martin squarely in the eyes. "I think you better lay this all out for us. What's really going on?"

Mom was watching him. Dad was watching him. "Okay. I know this is going to sound completely nuts. It sounds nuts to me when I think about it. It would sound one hundred percent mental to anyone, but what I'm going to tell you is absolutely the truth."

His parents still looked concerned, but they had also both added quizzical to the quality of their expressions. "Go on," his mother said. Dad interlaced his fingers and put his hands on the table. He was looking a little skeptical.

"Jack, the friend I mentioned. He's only sort of a friend. We met a couple weeks ago and he's not someone I really trust."

"Then you shouldn't be friends," Mom said.

"Hang on," Martin replied. "I don't entirely trust him because of the stories about him. See, he, uh . . . The stories about him are all how he tricked the devil and ended up cursed to walk the darkness."

Dad leaned forward in his chair, eyes wide. "Your friend is Stingy Jack?"

"Stingy Jack?" his mother asked.

"The guy from the origin of the jack-o'-lantern story. Buster asked me about him, about the story, a couple weeks ago."

"Only, it isn't a story. I asked you about him because I've met him. Well, he came to me . . . not like in a dream. In a pumpkin. He told me about his problem. Our problem—all of us. The whole world. And he told me we're his kin."

Dad cocked an eyebrow, "Kin? I think that little tidbit would have been passed down through the family, don't you?"

"Well..." Mom said. "Actually—"

Dad smacked his own forehead and said, "Seriously?"

"When we went to visit one Thanksgiving, great-grandad was telling stories. He told us a story his grandad told *him* about an uncle named Jack. I only heard him tell the story once. It never came up again. There could be something in the trunk in the attic."

Before Dad could respond, there was a loud "caw" from somewhere out in the yard. It drew both of their attention. It drew wide eyes from Martin.

Chapter 20

Dad was no longer sitting at the table with his fingers interlaced resting before him. He was no longer standing behind his chair with his hands placed across the top of its back. He had taken to pacing a small circuit, about three yards, a good bit of the width of the dining room. Mom couldn't decide whether to sit or stand.

In the conversation she and her husband had about this very meeting, there was no scenario in which their son declared the fate of the world was in his hands. They had not rehearsed a single response for finding out their son talked to ghosts. There was one point Dad couldn't get past. It was not, in the grand scheme of things, the most consequential detail, but it's the one he kept returning to. "Stingy Jack, the character from the Irish folktale . . . some 200 years old, is my in-law?"

This assumed that the story Martin had told them was real. It assumed there were ghosts that visited their home, and that the ghost calling himself Jack was telling the truth. There were a lot of assumptions. It was also beginning to bother Martin's mother this was the thing his father was hung up on.

"Sweetheart, can we return to that part later? I think maybe we want to talk about the rest of the story and what it is Martin says he needs to do." Mom's voice was up about an octave higher than usual. She was smiling and nodding and trying to hide the fact she was freaking out. She sat. "Buster, honey. This is quite the story."

Martin nodded and said, "I know it."

"Are you sure it isn't just a story though? I know sometimes it's easier to make up a story than to face the truth. Has something happened that you are having a hard time telling us? Something that would make you come up with all this stuff about ghosts and veils and other worlds?"

Martin chuckled, mostly to himself, and said, "Mom, what possibly could have happened in my life that what I've told you is a reasonable cover-up story for?"

Dad looked at Mom, held one hand out toward his boy, and waved it around a little. Martin wasn't sure how to interpret the gesture, but he thought it might mean that his father was telling his mother that their son had a good point.

"Have you talked to Mrs. Elliott about this?" Mom asked.

"Mrs. Elliott? The school counselor? No. I haven't. As far as I know, she doesn't have any expertise in the paranormal."

"Don't get smart, Buster," his father said.

"Listen. Listen. I told you it was going to sound crazy. I did. I warned you. You wanted me to tell you what's going on and you started asking a lot of specific questions and I have told you the truth. I know you have to accept that before you can even consider what it all means and this thing I need to do."

Neither of his parents said anything.

"What if I could prove it to you?"

Now, they both cocked their heads slightly. Dad raised an eyebrow.

Martin continued. "If I could prove that what I have told you is true, will you skip over the part where you get my head examined and put me in therapy and the part where you ask me if I'm taking drugs?"

"I . . . I don't know. I suppose if you could prove it . . ." Dad said, unsure.

"Yes," Mom said with surprising certainty. "You prove that this is not some strange game or elaborate fantasy and we will accept it as truth and move on to helping you with whatever you need to do." She looked Martin's father directly in the eye and nodded at him. He nodded back.

Martin took a deep breath. He sat up straight in his chair and hoped he'd been right in the assumption he'd made before their conversation had really begun. Rising and going across the dining room, he held his breath. He opened the window wide, then the storm window behind it. His mother said,

"Martin, what are you doing? You'll let the heat out." Martin ignored her.

"Charlie!" Martin called. "Charlie, if you're out there, please come to the window. I thought I heard you earlier. It's fine. My parents know."

He stepped away from the window and went to the front door. He opened it to find Lilith already waiting just a few feet beyond. "Come on in," he said. "Meet my parents."

Lilith followed Martin into the dining room, sat beside a chair, looked up at it and meowed. Martin asked his parents, "Do you mind if she sits in the chair?" His mother just stared at her son and the black cat who had sauntered into their living room.

Dad hunted a moment for words before coming up with, "Yeah. No. Sure. Sit."

A great flapping of wings beat a gust of chilly air into the dining room and a great, pitch black raven landed on the window sill. Martin's mother staggered back a step. "Boy . . . they're bigger . . . he's bigger than I thought they were." To Martin, Charlie appeared to bow. It probably looked to his parents like he was just doing some bird thing.

"Ask him to be careful of the wood please, Martin," Dad said. But before Martin conveyed the message, Charlie adjusted his talons so they weren't biting into the window sill. "Did he . . . did he understand me?"

Charlie looked to Martin and Martin nodded his head.

Charlie spoke. "I did understand you. Yes. I'm sure this must all come as a very great shock, and I apologize for that. Nevertheless, it is a pleasure to meet you. My friends have taken to calling me Charlie and I would be pleased if you would, too."

After staring, dumb, at the great bird for several long seconds, Mom and Dad turned to face the cat who was now sitting in a dining room chair. Martin nodded to her. She said, "I'm Lilith. It's nice to meet you, and thank you for allowing us into your home."

Martin looked at his parents and said, "She's actually been living, or at least spending a lot of time, under the front porch since this all started."

"So many questions," Mom said.

"Yes. Cats and ravens can talk, though I think most would agree they'd rather ravens did not. If people knew we could it would simply cause too much upheaval."

Mom said nothing. Dad nodded and said, "Right."

Charlie said, "Also, yes, we do live in both this world and the others. I assume that is one of the other questions you have."

"And, yes, this world is in trouble because of an imbalance of a power that appears to be connected to fear. We've taken to calling it Jack-o'-Lightning," Lilith added.

Dad was still nodding. He seemed to have turned into a bobble head. Mom was running her fingers through her hair. Martin had only seen her do that when she was really tired or really stressed out. He was betting on the latter.

* * *

"I'm sorry," Charlie said. "I don't mean to be presumptuous. It's just the questions about us talking and where we're really from, are almost always the first. I'm sure you have others, and I will do . . . we will do our best to answer them."

"Hang on!" Martin said. "I'm sure my parents have lots of questions and I know they want to ask them, but I have one first. You're back and that means, I hope, that you learned something."

"I did," Charlie said, shifting his weight from one foot to the other and back again.

"And?" Martin said.

"And it is as Gump suggested." Charlie turned to Martin's parents. "Gump is a goblin. I have known him for some time, but he is a recent acquaintance of Lilith and your son."

"Okay," Mom managed to say.

Charlie went on. "There are artifacts, relics, if you will, that seem to pulse with the lightning. The rider has been hoarding them, gathering them from all over the other worlds and sending thieves into this one to steal them. He's got them hidden all over."

"That's got to be one of the ways the other side had gathered so much power," Martin said.

"I suspect that's part of it," Lilith added. "He also could simply be hoarding them to keep their power away from this side."

Martin's parents both sat down, not saying a word but watching and listening to the conversation intently.

Lilith continued, "We know some of the shift in balance is the decline of humans' interest in what lies on the other side. People aren't as curious. They aren't as scared. They don't tap on the veil like they once did. And the things they do fear don't generate the same kind of power."

Charlie said, "Fearing one another is not the same thing as fearing the things that go bump in the night."

"Just so. That kind of fear feeds some of those on the other side. They can use it," said Lilith.

"But these relics, they have to help, right?" Martin said.

"Oh, I'm sure they do," Charlie said. "And there are quite a few of them from what my conspiracy tells me."

Martin turned to his parents, "That's what a group of ravens is called."

Again, Mom managed an "Okay."

Charlie went on, "They seem to know where some of them are. At least they have an idea of the areas to look in. Unfortunately, he doesn't keep them in a glass case marked 'powerful relics' on display anywhere obvious."

"Of course not," Dad said, earning him a sideways glance from his wife.

"But, your friends . . . er . . . family . . . they could get me close?"

"I think so. You would need a guide, though, someone who could get you the rest of the way, follow the trail. It wouldn't hurt if this guide was skilled in the art of stealth. You might need help slipping in and out of places you shouldn't be."

Lilith stopped grooming herself and stared at Charlie, her eyes alight with the reflection of the dining room chandelier.

"I shouldn't be in the underworld at all," Martin said, and his mother and father both nodded their heads.

"I can't say I disagree, but you know what's at stake," Charlie said.

Martin swallowed hard and said, "I do."

"So this guide," Charlie continued, but was interrupted.

"Are you intentionally being thick or are you just doing your feathered finest to ignore the obvious answer and get a rise out of me?"

Charlie didn't answer.

"I knew he meant you," Martin said.

"But he wasn't about to come out and say it."

Martin turned to his parents and said, "They kind of have a thing, cats and ravens. I didn't know that until a few days ago. It's not pretty."

"But," Charlie cawed, "we are listening to the angels of our better nature and working together. Though many ravens are neutral on the matter and some are well in favor of the rider's plan, I have decided to throw my lot in with your son."

"Thanks," Dad said, but it sounded more like a question.

Martin asked, "You say there are a lot of these relics. How do I know which to take? Do I just grab the first one we find?"

"Given what my kin have told me, I have some ideas about that," Charlie said.

Chapter 21

The conversation at the dining room table didn't last much beyond the conversation of the relics, but as it continued, Martin's parents seemed to adjust, or begin to adjust, to what they were seeing and hearing. When Charlie left, but before Martin had closed the window, Mom and Dad called behind him, "Nice to meet you, Charlie. Thank you for helping our son." Even they seemed a little surprised to be saying it, but Martin was glad they did.

They turned to Lilith after that and Mom said, "We aren't really set up for a cat. I mean, we don't have a litter box or any cat food in the house."

"I appreciate the thought, but I've been fine under the porch and there are other cozy places to curl up in the neighborhood."

Dad said, "But it's chilly out there. Why don't you stay in here, and if you need to go out, let Martin know and he can let you into the yard?" He chuckled and added, "Since you're talking to us, we don't need to worry about trying to figure out what you're saying if you paw at the door."

Lilith stretched her back, flexing her toes on both front paws and said, "I sincerely appreciate your hospitality."

Once he and his mom had set out a blanket at the end of Martin's bed for Lilith to sleep on, and he had brushed his teeth and gotten himself ready for bed, Martin composed a text message. "Dale, I know you said you'd contact me if you thought of anything, and I am sorry to bother you, but I wanted to let you know that I am going to travel to the other side of the veil to try and find an artifact that might help shift the balance of Jack-o'-Lightning. There were several things we could seek out, but I'm after one that might make you think a little more about your writing. If the information my friend received is true, I'm going after the last quill of Edgar Allan Poe."

* * *

Dale read the message several times over. There was obviously a great deal to the story Martin had left out. He was okay with that for the time being at least. He disapproved of text messages that were several pages long. Martin was crossing the veil. Dale hoped that didn't mean Martin was dying, or taking his own life. Evidently, he was going in search of one of several possible relics, namely the last quill of Edgar Allan Poe. As a one-time dabbler in horror writing, Dale could think of far worse talismans of the power he and Martin had spoken of, of the power he had come to feel on those couple occasions when he had written. Dale wasn't sure how having Poe's quill would help Martin's plight, much less how he was going to get it, but the boy was determined. That much was certain.

He put his phone down on the kitchen counter and eyed the copper kettle on the stove, willing it to boil so he could have a cup of tea. Tea helped him think. It helped him unwind. He'd picked up the habit from his grandmother when he was a teenager. If he needed to talk to someone, to clear his head, or get something out, he would sit at his grandmother's kitchen table and she'd make them both peppermint tea. He thought it was time for a cup.

Dale had been thinking about Martin when the boy's message arrived. There wasn't any evidence, no clear explanation of how his writing related to this "Jack-o'-Lightning"—and he felt as though he'd done the right thing for himself by closing the door on that part of his life—but he couldn't help feeling as though he'd abandoned Martin.

So, when the tea kettle whistled and he'd fixed his cup, instead of sitting with it at the kitchen table as he was accustomed to doing, he carried it up the stairs to the little room that served as his office, and placed it on his desk. He was breaking all the rules. It wasn't the extra hour of Daylight Savings Time. It wasn't even dark out. He simply wasn't a writer, but for lack of any other way he could help, he knew he had to do it. If everything Martin had told him was true—though he hoped it was a gross exaggeration—he simply could not sit by and watch. Dale opened his notebook and began to write.

Chapter 22

"I'm really not at all comfortable with this," Martin's mother said to his father.

"Neither am I, but I think we've seen enough to know that it's all real."

"Real or not, why does it have to be our boy?" Martin's mom was changing into her pajamas while his father was brushing his teeth.

He said through a foam of toothpaste. "I don't know. Maybe it doesn't. But there doesn't seem to be anyone else. And if the world—"

"If the world is going to end, there's no time to waste. Is that what you were going to say?"

Dad spit into the sink and rinsed his mouth out with a bit of tap water. "Something like that, yes."

"We don't know how much time there is."

Dad said, "I think Halloween is a safe bet. You know, the ancient Celts believed that Samhain was the time the veil was the thinnest, and they were—I suppose—much more connected to all that than we are now."

"Okay, so we have until Halloween to find someone else to do this," Mom said.

"I don't think so. Honey, I don't like any of this either. We don't know if it's possible, but if Halloween is the final day—the day when all this could happen—Martin needs to try this plan before that. Then, if it doesn't work, we have time to come up with a Plan B."

"Let's start working on a Plan B right now," Mom said.

Dad replied, "I'm open to suggestions. I am sure Buster would be, too. You seemed a lot more okay with all this downstairs." He had changed into his pajamas and climbed between the flannel sheets on their queen-sized bed. Mom was sitting on her side of the bed, fingers to her eyes, removing her contacts.

She said, "I wasn't okay with it. I don't know. Maybe it just hadn't sunk in yet. Maybe I was just wishing Jack wasn't my great-stinking-uncle! I was a little shocked and not really taking in that we were talking about our son travelling to the underworld, slipping among ghosts and demons with a cat leading the way, to steal Edgar Allan Poe's quill away from the headless horseman."

Dad was silent for a moment. He had to admit it sounded absolutely horrifying when she strung it together out loud like that, but he was also proud, and that made him feel a little guilty. It was his son that might be about to save the world. It was his son who was brave enough to face this seemingly impossible, surreal task. He felt as though he shouldn't be thinking about it like that, that he should be focused on his child's safety and getting him out of the mess he was in, and that brought on the guilt.

Mom said, "What are you thinking? You got a little far off just now. Is it too much to hope you had an idea?"

"Afraid not," he replied, reaching for the switch for the bedroom lights. "If I dream one up, I'll wake you."

"It's not funny," Mom said.

"I wasn't joking. I love you, honey. Try to get some sleep. We'll talk more in the morning." He leaned over and they shared a gentle goodnight kiss before closing their eyes and wishing for sleep.

* * *

Martin was in his room down the hall, tossing things onto his bed and listing them off as he did. "Hat. Gloves. Scarf. T-shirt in case it gets hot. Extra sweater in case it gets cold. Flash Light. Extra batteries."

Lilith, sitting on the end of his bed, said, "I don't know if that will work over there. I've never actually seen anyone carry one."

"I guess we'll find out," Martin replied. "Should I bring a first aid kit? Dad has one in the garage."

"It couldn't hurt."

"I'm bringing my cell phone, but I'm thinking they don't have the same service providers over there. Maybe I'll need pictures or . . . I don't know."

"Did you pack any food?"

"I'm hoping not to be there long enough to need to eat, but I should probably get a snack or two. And water."

"Yes, I think that's wise. I don't know what it will be like for you. We're creatures of both sides—cats—so it probably all works differently for you than for us, and I haven't known any humans personally who have crossed."

"And I'm thinking we don't want to raise any suspicions or draw any attention by asking around for a place to get a drink."

"No."

Martin stuffed everything but the bottle of water and snacks, which he'd grab in the kitchen on his way out, into his backpack and slung the pack over his shoulder. He had decided that he needed to go as quickly as he could. He didn't want his mother and father to have time to try and stop him. They knew what he had to do and they would know where he was if they woke and he was gone.

He slipped out the back door as silently as he could manage and ran across the back yard into the wood.

* * *

Jack was waiting in the darkness where Lilith said he'd be. He was there but not there, a kind of heavy mist vaguely in the shape of a man. In one hand he carried a turnip which appeared far more substantial than it had the last time Martin had seen it. It appeared more substantial than Jack himself. The walls of the turnip were scorched, as was a circular spot at the base where rested a small black coal—but there was no flame. Jack silently held the dark lantern out to Martin.

Martin took it and held it up in front of his face. He stared at it, turned it one way and then around the other. This was the first jack-o'-lantern. This

119

was the very object that started a centuries-old Halloween tradition, and he was holding it in his hand. Martin was thinking of how the folklore was, in fact, the truth, when he was jarred from his reverie by the realization of how insubstantial Jack had become and wondered what he had done—or was about to do.

Lilith wove in and out between Jack's invisible legs, and he made no move to shoo her off. He turned hollow-looking sockets to Martin's wide eyes and said, with a mouth that was barely there, "If this works, then we save your world. If it doesn't, then we fail the world and I cease to exist in either."

"We don't know—"

"No, we don't. We don't know what's going to happen and that's terrifying, lad. This could be the very end of me."

"Why? What are you going to do?"

"It took nearly everything I had to make the lantern corporeal again. I've nearly burned out the devil's coal in the process. I'm going to replace it."

"Replace it?" said Lilith.

"Aye. I become the lantern. Martin, you can open the veil with it, there and back—as I do when I slip through—and carry it . . . me across. Just look where you want it to open and hold out the lantern in that direction. I'll be your light, and it might keep me from being spotted on the other side. I don't know."

Martin said, "But you can . . . come back out again, right—once we cross back to this side? We could scare up the energy you need, I'm sure."

"We could, m'boy. We could. I appreciate your optimism. I suppose I could just end up trapped in this old turnip for the rest of time, too. Have I told you, after centuries of carrying it around, I really hate turnips."

Martin smiled. "I don't blame you. Ready?"

"No. Nor will I ever be, but let's do this, nonetheless."

Lilith backed up several steps. Martin held the lantern at arm's length. Jack, or the mist in nearly the shape of Jack, curled in on itself and condensed. It swirled, slowly at first, then quickly enough to turn up a short gust that riffled Lilith's fur. Where Jack's feet would have been, the glow lifted from the ground and narrowed to a point smaller than Martin's fist. It floated towards the turnip lantern and into the hollow. The rest of the Jack-mist followed until all of him had disappeared inside, a nearly solid ball of swirling energy.

Lilith meowed. Martin held his breath. For several long moments, nothing happened. There was no sound, no change in the motion, no flash. Martin inspected the turnip closer and could see nothing different. He knelt down and showed it to Lilith, who sniffed at it.

"It smells like him," she said.

And then the coal began to glow. It was just the slightest of lights at first, but it was there. Martin beamed. "Look!" he said and showed Lilith again. They watched intently as the little glow grew. It was growing even as the mist dispersed and the light grew brighter. It was no camp lantern, no D-cell battery-powered beacon. It cast light only a few feet in every direction, but that it cast light at all meant that it had worked.

"Jack?" Martin said.

There was no reply.

"Jack," he said again.

There was no audible answer, but Martin was certain the coal had surged a little brighter for just an instant. It was enough for him to decide their plan had worked.

Lilith trotted past Martin a few feet deeper into the wood and meowed. Martin looked to see where she had wandered to when he noticed it.

There was a shimmer in the air, like the space above blacktop in mid-July. It stretched in both directions as far as he could see. It ran from the ground into the dark night sky. There was no door, no gate, no guard. There was simply a shimmer. He could see the woods beyond it. They looked like his woods, the ones he knew well, where he played with friends and went for walks with his parents. There was nothing sinister-looking about them, at least no more so than dark woods ever look.

"Is that it?" Martin asked.

"The veil," Lilith said.

III

Part Three

Chapter 23

Martin walked towards the shimmer. There was nothing left to do but cross through it. "Will it look like this when I come back?" he asked.

"More or less. Don't worry. I'll lead you back."

Martin scoffed at the idea of not worrying. He was travelling to a place you're only supposed to travel to when you're dead. He was only going into hostile territory where the headless horseman was taking over worlds and gathering power. He stopped himself from riding that train of thought. It only served to weaken his knees and shorten his steps.

There was only one more before one of his feet was on the other side of the shimmer. He took a deep breath, which caught in his throat, and placed his right foot in front of his left. At first, Martin could see no difference. It was a dark wood, maybe a little darker than before, but he thought that could just be his mind playing tricks on him. The trees were tall and barren, but they were trees no different from his own woods: birch, maple, and oak. There was a cold breeze he didn't remember being on the other side, but mostly the place was the same.

"Did we cross over?" he asked Lilith.

"We did. You can't feel it?"

"No. I don't feel anything other than a little cold."

Lilith padded through the thick layer of downed leaves and Martin followed. He hadn't made it more than twenty yards when the first evidence he was not in his world was clear. There was a howl, as if a hundred wolves or more chose the same moment to plead with the moon. It reverberated off the trees and seemed to multiply and echo rather than fade. The black cat guide paused a moment, looked over her shoulder at Martin and continued.

"What was that?" he whisper-shouted to her.

"It's hard to say," she replied. "There're all sorts over here, remember, and sorts from all kinds of worlds."

"We aren't heading towards that sound, are we?"

"Not on your life," she said.

They continued walking. It was the sounds that continued to separate these woods from any he'd know before. There were howls like the first. There were no crickets. There were caws, screeches, and hoots. There were things that scurried and slithered. The more he listened, the more noises there seemed to be. He twisted to face one way, then the other, then behind him, always holding the lantern before him to see what he could see, but it was all shadows and sounds.

The moon had risen high but cast little light through the trees. It seemed to Martin it was the wrong color. It wasn't white. It wasn't orange like a harvest moon or even red like the blood moon he'd seen a year or so before. It was a sickly shade of yellow, it seemed to him, but he couldn't focus on it long enough to settle on a description. It looked impossibly far away and his eyes strained to see it.

Lilith doubled back to walk alongside her companion. He'd fallen a little behind as he searched and scanned their path. "We aren't far," she said.

"From?"

"The edge of the wood. Well, unless Jack and his lantern have now cursed you to do his job for him."

The small glow from inside the turnip flared a moment, but Martin didn't know what it meant. It could be denial. It could be an admission. It could be a laugh that he'd tricked another. Martin chose to believe it was denial. It was the only possibility that lessened his terror.

"What's on the other side of the wood?" Martin asked.

"Well," replied Lilith, "it should be a clearing."

"Should be?"

"Things do change around here. I think it's because the borders between worlds have gotten fuzzy and one place ebbs and flows into another. There is usually a clearing around these woods, though. We'll cross that and head into the hills. The raven said he'd meet us or have someone meet us near the trail in that direction. I admit I don't know exactly where he means, but I suppose we'll find out."

"Charlie," Martin said.

"What?"

"His name is Charlie."

"Fine. Charlie."

They walked on.

* * *

By the time Lilith and Martin had come within spotting distance of the clearing, word had reached the rider there was a human in his realm, but word hadn't come from the Keeper. The Keeper had felt it but chose to ignore the itch that came from it. He had no interest in Jack's business and knew it was only Jack who could have come back across and caused the itch. Besides, he had no intention of aiding the rider after their last meeting.

The bats and snakes of the wood had noticed, but took no interest. The coyotes prowled with watchful eyes. These were not the creatures who slunk off to the rider to give report. It was the ghouls and ghasts who feared his reprisal if they didn't report what they had seen. They coveted his power. They yearned for the freedom he'd promised them. And many of them simply resented and despised the living.

The rider had been in his home, a stone keep that once sat just inside the border to the realm of the Fae folk. News came in whispers from unseen mouths.

"A human. In the woods. A cat with him. And something more." It was a hissing, breathless multitude of voices. The rider sat straight in his chair, lifted the flaming pumpkin off the heavy table before him and placed it on his shoulders.

"What more?" he demanded.

"A spirit."

"There are untold hordes of spirits. What concern is it of mine if there is a spirit with the human. It's the human I care about. What is he doing? How did he come?"

"The spirit," whispered the voice, "The spirit is familiar. It carried a lantern—a turnip lantern."

Dozens of hairy-legged spiders skittered up the arms of the rider's claimed throne and dropped from the rafters over his head. In their collective voice they whispered, "Jack. It's he and the boy we told you about, the boy and horrid cat. "

"A human walks my lands with Jack of the lantern and a feline?" The rider stood. "You say they are in the wood? What wood? Where?"

"In the forest. Near the forest. Near the hills. The black forest to the east."

"What more do you know?"

"Nothing, master."

"Leave me. I must ride." The voices came no more as the headless horseman stalked from his keep. Beyond its gate, his great, black mount waited, pacing and snorting. The beast had become an extension of the rider himself. Though it took directions from the rider when given, it needed none. It went where he needed it to go. So, when the rider was in the saddle, the horse didn't wait for a command; it turned towards the east and set out at a gallop.

Chapter 24

Martin had imagined a clearing as being a place where the trees broke, where sunlight came through during the day and moonlight at night. A clearing was a place where grass grew, and wildflowers, in his own world. What he stepped out into was no kind of clearing he'd pictured. Though there were no trees he could see from where he stood, save those at his back, there was no grass, no wildflowers, and it was only brighter by a fraction. He didn't expect to see deer looking for a snack as they sometimes did in a clearing in the woods at home. Of course, he thought, there could be other things than deer.

Here, the ground was barren, cracked, and in some places appeared scorched. There were great holes that appeared as though something had dug out from beneath the earth or burrowed into it from above. There were smaller holes that reminded Martin of snakes or small rodents. Lilith said nothing of them, but Martin noticed her ears were further back against her head and the hairs at the base of her neck were slightly raised.

"Are we safe?" Martin asked.

"Hardly ever," Lilith replied.

"That's comforting."

"It's the truth."

"So, you have no idea where we're going once we reach these hills?" Martin could just make out a rolling change in the terrain on the horizon.

"Some idea, but not specifically, no. The raven—sorry—Charlie didn't give me a lot of detail. He just said we'd have help when we got that far."

They walked on. The sounds of the wood faded behind them, but the new sounds were somehow worse. They were too strange a blend, and they set

Martin's hair on end. From one direction he could faintly hear wails and screaming and from another music from instruments he didn't recognize; something like a flute, he thought, and a whistle. He couldn't focus on one sound at a time to identify its source. There was laughter, but there was also angry shouting in languages foreign to his ear.

The woods had smelled like woods, earthy, rich, a little damp. The clearing smelled burnt. It smelled like wood smoke with something tinny behind it, like someone was burning leaves but also scrap they'd pulled from the garage. He could see smoke in the air. It was far off and wispy, but in the dark, Martin thought it must be a large fire for the smoke to still be seen from a distance.

"You don't notice the smells after a while," Lilith said. She had paused and sat several yards ahead of Martin and had been watching him as he tried to take in his environment.

"I'm pretty sure I don't want to know what I'm smelling," he said.

Lilith replied, "It could be things you've never imagined. It's safer just to focus on something else?"

"Like the scenic beauty?" Martin smiled, though he wasn't feeling as jovial as the smile he offered might suggest.

"There was beauty in some of these worlds. There still is. You just have to travel awhile to find it."

"And what was this world? What is this world we're in now?"

"I suppose it's a kind of no-man's-land. It's a part of the realm of the dead."

"Shouldn't it be full of them, then? Spirits, I mean—the dead?"

Lilith began walking again. She said, "It is. You just haven't noticed them because most of them don't want you to. Be glad of that. Many of the dead don't much care for the living."

Martin paused and looked around him again, holding the lantern before him. He saw no spirits, but now that Lilith had said what she had, he thought he noticed little ripples in the air, little shadows where there was nothing to cast them. He wondered if it was possible in a place like this to know if you could trust your eyes, or if you were losing your mind.

The terrain began shifting. Their path had followed a persistent, gentle, upward slope since they'd left the wood, but there was starting to be a noticeable roll beneath their feet. Ahead of them—and just off what passed for the trail they were walking—was what appeared to be an old church. It looked like the kind of place that couldn't be more than a sanctuary and a small room or two, perhaps a closet. In another world, it might have been white, the steeple crowned with a cross, and stained glass in its window. Here it was the deep grey of old wood, with no adornment.

Not one exterior wall was perfectly perpendicular to the ground. There had once been a steeple where now there was simply a pile of rubble heaped on the steeply canted roof. The door was either open to the inside or missing. On the other side of the door, windows without glass were framed by broken and sagging shutters.

"Could our help be in there?" Martin asked.

"Could be."

"Should we look?"

Lilith sniffed at the air. "I'm not picking up anything more awful than this place usually offers."

"Can you scout ahead?"

Lilith bobbed her head, lowered her body a little closer to the earth and sped towards the dilapidated structure. Moments later she returned at a normal gait and told Martin, "There's no threat that I can tell, but no contact either."

"Let's check it out anyway." Martin hoped the contact would be there, would arrive when they were near. He needed there to be direction, instructions he could follow. He also didn't like being out in the open. He felt exposed. He felt like he was being watched. So, they walked another few dozen yards and crossed the threshold of what might once have been a church.

Chapter 25

Martin was glad the building was only one floor. He didn't trust that they wouldn't fall through if they'd been standing anywhere but at ground level. The barn had been dark. The church was something else altogether. A puddle of light spilled from the lantern but could not pierce the black. Lilith guided Martin to the far end of the sanctuary, where the melted nubs of candles still had the suggestion of a wick.

Martin held the lantern over the candles, prepared to coax enough of a flame to light them. He didn't have to blow on the coal like he'd expected. He tipped the lantern towards the candles and a lick of flame bent towards them and brought them sputtering to life. "Thanks Jack," Martin said, and looked around for more waxy stumps.

There turned out to be a half dozen candles on what had probably once been an altar. Even all lit, they cast only enough light to make the whole of the high-ceilinged sanctuary dimly visible. It was as the outside had been: graying wood and disrepair. There was a thick layer of dust on the pews, and the pulpit had fallen on its side.

"Why is there a church out here?" Martin asked.

Lilith, sniffing around the room, said, "Hard to say. I suppose it was built by the dead. Maybe it was here from another world. Maybe it exists somewhere on the other side and this is a shadow of that place. As I said, Martin, the rules here are different. You shouldn't expect things to make sense. The reasons for things existing, or being the way they are, may defy any explanation that would make sense to you."

Martin said nothing in return. He continued to look around the room, hoping that something would make sense, hoping that somewhere in this abandoned place he'd find a clue, uncover a secret, learn a trick for navigating the unsettling world he'd traveled to.

"Lovely, isn't it?" came a voice from the shadow high above.

Lilith growled long and low.

"Now, that's not at all necessary."

Martin looked nervously at Lilith. She rumbled a moment longer and said, "Raven."

This development didn't please her. The appearance of one of her sworn rivals never would, but Martin's pulse quickened with excitement. "I'm Martin," he said into the darkness.

A raven—a head smaller than Charlie—circled down from the rafters to perch on a pew. "I assumed as much. There aren't a multitude of humans wandering around these days, even fewer children with a cat in tow."

His tone wasn't like Charlie's at all. The small hairs on Martin's arms stood up. "Are you a friend of Charlie's?"

The raven croaked and stomped its talons on the pew. It was the same sound as what he'd learned was Charlie's laugh, but it was louder and longer and Martin was even less comfortable with it than Charlie's. "Friend is a strong word. We don't keep friends, you see. A conspiracy is safety. It's numbers. We're a family by species and some by blood, but friendship is special and rare. The one you call Charlie is known to me. We have spoken.

Lilith sat on her haunches, eyes fixed on the great black bird. "Did he send you to find us?"

"I am not *sent* anywhere. We do not order one another about."

"Sorry," Martin said. "Did he ask you to help us?"

"He asked."

"And are you going to?" Martin asked, trying to swallow the growing lump at the back of his throat.

"I could," the raven said. "I could. Then again, I could tell the rider where you are. He might reward me. He's coming, you know? Others have already told him you were here and in which direction you might be found."

Martin's knees felt weak. He was afraid to say anything lest the fear in his voice betray him. The bird was trying to scare him, to put him off guard, and he knew he couldn't let it see that it was working.

Fortunately for him, Lilith stepped in. "You could do either thing. I can't see a gain for you either way. What reward does the rider have that he could give a raven?"

The raven cocked its head. "What reward might a cat or a human child have?"

"None," Lilith said and the bird cocked its head again. Martin was stunned. He thought maybe they needed a moment to think about it, come up with an offer, strategize, and plan, but Lilith continued, "We ask the favor as Charlie did. We are trying to save the boy's world. Does helping the rider cost you anything? Does the rider offer anything your conspiracy wants? Do you lack for land to survey or places to perch? Do you lack for food?"

The raven hopped from one foot to the next. He cocked his head one direction, then the other. Martin recognized this as a thinking gesture. The raven was considering.

Lilith said, "The choice isn't about a kindness for us or a favor to the rider. The question is: Is there a right thing to do?"

The raven cawed, loud and echoing through the old church. "What do I care about the right thing?"

"You aren't evil," Martin said. "You might be intimidating, but you aren't evil."

"The rider *is* evil," Lilith said.

"And he doesn't care about you unless you serve him," Martin was taking a gamble. The ravens were proudly, fiercely independent.

"We serve no master," the bird said. "We serve no one."

"Then help us or leave us be. Going to him only offers your services. He will see you as messengers he can use," Lilith said, hopping onto the pew a few feet from the raven.

The raven had heard that the rider recently approached his kin about being his eyes and ears between the worlds. None of them had paid it much mind. They had no intention of going out of their way to do favors. The consensus had been to stay away from his business altogether. The large bird flapped his wings and took to the shutters, mostly hidden by the shadows. Martin and Lilith gazed up after him.

"Through the hills to the river. Cross before it turns white. Continue east until you reach the stones. Then look north for the village. You'll find what you seek near there. Now go. The dead will soon return to their worship and they will not hesitate to share your location with the horseman."

Martin exchanged looks with Lilith. He wanted to ask what dangers to watch for, if there were trails or trials they would meet along the way, but he didn't get the chance. The raven cawed another of its fierce calls and said again, "Go." They left the church and walked briskly east, further into the hills.

* * *

They heard before they saw the river. It sounded like any other Martin had heard. It was the sound of moving water, bubbling along its route, carrying debris, and paying no mind to the banks it slowly eroded. Martin wondered if the calm sound of a slowly running river would be the same in any world, but remembered what Lilith had said and thought that in some worlds a river could sound like screams and in another a music box.

They crested a hill and gazed down upon a river that looked nothing like what it had sounded like. It was moving swiftly. It was carrying debris, as most rivers do, but the debris was not branches and leaves. The debris appeared to be bones and hard-to-define shapes that might once have been living things. There wasn't much of it, but any at all was enough to turn Martin's stomach. "Tell me the river isn't blood," he said.

"No. We'd smell it if it was."

They walked a little ways further and Martin grew more certain that what flowed was in fact water, though it appeared streaked with oil that reflected the moon's sickly pallor. "How do we cross?" He asked.

Lilith looked up and down the river and saw no bridge, no boat, no conveyance or path of any kind. "He said to cross before it turns white. I guess we follow it awhile and see what we can find."

Martin could think of no better plan, so they walked along. The moon had crossed its zenith and appeared to be on its way towards setting, though Martin didn't know how long it would take, nor was he sure that the sun would follow, but he hoped that whatever came next cast more light. The inky blackness was beginning to sap his strength and, with it, his courage. As they walked, he slung his backpack around under one arm and removed the extra sweater. He wanted to take a sip from his water bottle, but he let go of it as he looked towards the river, water not feeling particularly appetizing just then.

Chapter 26

After a quick search of each room, and a circuit of the yard, calling his name and casting the beams of flashlights into the darkness, Martin's parents were in full crisis mode.

"Maybe he went into the woods. He said he talked to Stingy Jack there once."

"In the middle of the night?" Mom was pacing the front porch, continuing to shine her flashlight into the darkness.

"Maybe that's how it works. Maybe it has to be under the moon or something."

"No. You know where he is. We both know where he is. He went to the other world. He's gone."

Dad paced behind mom, his hand lightly rubbing her back. He knew she was probably right. "Do you think he would have told anyone he was going?"

"It's possible, but I didn't see his phone anywhere to check. Did you?"

"No." Dad was silent for another circuit of the porch before adding, "His laptop is upstairs, though."

When Mom didn't immediately reply, he said, "He might have sent someone a message, you know, like on Facebook or Twitter or something."

"Do you know his passwords?" Mom asked.

"I know his laptop password. Remember, we told him he had to give it to us . . . unless he's changed it." Dad couldn't help but think it was possible, given his son's recent secrecy. "I don't know about passwords for websites and things, though. I guess we have to hope he stays logged in."

Martin's parents had this exchange while ascending the stairs. Mom stood in a far corner of the boy's room, on the other side of the desk. Dad stood over the desk, bending to power up the laptop they'd bought him for his birthday the year before. The password was the same and Martin did stay logged in to a couple of social apps. The browser was already open with a couple of tabs across the top.

The first tab was his school's website, scrolled to a homework help area, and that made both Martin's parents proud. The next tab was some kind of video game sight featuring videos of people playing and advertising walkthroughs and hints. The final tab was the jackpot. It was a social media site with the chat window open.

"Who was he talking to?" Mom asked. "Is there anything there?"

"I'm looking," Dad said, clicking the history to see if there were any messages from that night. There was one. It was to Sidney. She hadn't replied because he'd sent his very late, Dad assumed. It confirmed what he and Mom had suspected. Martin had crossed to the other side.

"He's gone over," Dad said, closing the laptop.

Mom held her head in the palm of her hands and leaned against her husband. Neither of them said a word for a long time.

* * *

Sidney didn't get the message until the next morning. She read it, worried for Martin, and wished he'd waited until someone had come up with a way to help. She thought about calling him, texting him, or sending him a message, but knew she wouldn't be able to reach him.

Sidney did send a couple of messages before leaving for school that morning. One was to Chester. One was to Emmett. They read the same: "Martin has gone to the underworld. If you can think of anything, now is the time." She wasn't even entirely sure that was true, but she could think of nothing else to say. On the bus, she thought of a day not that long ago when she'd gone to school knowing, given the strange turn her life had taken, she was going to have a hard time focusing on her assignments. She knew *this* was going to be harder. She barely knew Martin, but she knew that he was taking a risk, an incredibly brave risk, that might or might not help save the world.

* * *

No one had told Baxter Martin was leaving. She hadn't been part of the conversation in the barn. She hadn't been brought in on the plan. For several days she'd grazed in various woods and parks around eastern Massachusetts, getting to know the locals and sampling the few plants that remained late in the season.

Baxter told herself that if someone needed her, she'd know. Reindeer have a bit of a sixth sense like that and, though she didn't exactly feel as though she'd been called to help, she did feel like something might be wrong. It was just unease at what could be at stake, she decided, and tried to ignore the tingle between her ears.

When she woke, on the morning after Martin had passed between worlds, she decided she had waited long enough and took off for Martin's house to see if there was any news.

* * *

Dale wasn't a writer—he was certain of that—but he knew writers. He had at least a passing familiarity with a few horror authors. A man had come to the local library once and he and Dale had struck up a conversation. The man introduced him to a couple of his fellows and, though he hadn't stayed in touch, he thought maybe they'd gotten on well enough they might remember him.

Somewhere in his desk he still had the contact information for the editor of Horrorpocolyse, assuming it hadn't changed and she was still with the publishing company. She might come in handy as well. Dale thought he might have the beginnings of a plan. He wasn't prepared to call it that just yet, but the more he rolled it around in his mind, the more peppermint tea he poured over it, the more he liked it.

He wasn't prepared to talk to Martin about it. He wouldn't tell the boy until—if—he put it all together, and he hadn't started the putting-it-together stage yet. Dale sat at his kitchen table with his old Rolodex and a notepad in front of him, and began to flip the cards.

* * *

With Lilith's help, Gump had developed a plan. He wasn't entirely satisfied with it, afraid it wasn't enough to generate the kind of power he felt they needed, but it was all he and Lilith had come up with in their brainstorming. He would start with small pranks—tricks that would attract the attention of older children and adolescents. Once engaged, he'd ask them to pull pranks of their own. He didn't want anyone getting hurt. He worried about kids taking the pranks too far, so he would be careful to explain the purpose was to startle and spook, not embarrass or injure.

The pranks needed to be planned for after dark on Halloween. In the meantime, he'd entice them to another bit of mischief. He wanted them to "pilfer pumpkins from a patch," and bring them to him. If they needed convincing, he was a master of pranks and would tease and trick them until they felt compelled to participate.

Lilith's contribution hadn't taken much to design. The idea had been raised when the group was still gathered in the barn. She would spread the word that it was the cats' time to shine. When she included the detail ravens would be pulling a stunt of their own, she knew recruitment wouldn't be difficult.

"Be creepy," she would say. "Be places you don't normally go. If you're outside, gather in places that would unsettle people—cemeteries, churchyards, outside schools in large groups. Yowl. Hiss. Arch your backs and spit."

She'd meet some resistance. Docile house cats would fear their people taking them to the vet in response to strange behavior, but that was okay. There were enough street cats—feral cats—they would not be lacking in numbers.

* * *

Charlie split his time between recruiting his brethren to the scare-cause, and soliciting rumors. The plan, as he explained it, was simple. There would be swarms, clouds, tornados of ravens and their nearest relations. Each conspiracy, each flock, each murder of crows would decide how to best execute their task. Their only job was to instill fear and wonder.

Many of those Charlie approached had no interest. They had no allegiance to one side of the veil or the other, and so no reason to participate. When he explained to them that the cats of the world would be trying to outshine them, nearly every bird he spoke to was eager to do its part.

Charlie's hunt for rumors returned little detail. Martin and Lilith, and possibly Jack, had been spotted. They'd crossed at least two or three lands. The rider was aware of them and on the move. There was nothing Charlie could do on either side of the veil to protect the boy. The best he could offer was to gather what information he could and share it with Martin's friends and family on this side.

Chapter 27

The land had begun to slope downward as they walked along the river, staying safely away from the banks. The river was slowly, almost imperceptibly, picking up speed, and Lilith had pointed out that before long it would start to turn white with foam as it rushed over rocks, assuming that's what the raven had meant. Martin was anxious for a place to cross, though he did not look forward to the crossing. Whether by bridge or watercraft, he was not enthusiastic about being on that river. He did want it behind them, though.

"I don't suppose we could find this village we're looking for by going through another world, could we? Maybe Candy Land, or the World of Sunshine and Pixie Dust."

Lilith shook her head. "I'm not sure if those worlds exist. Besides, it would just add steps if we had to travel overland through Big Rock Candy Mountain."

Martin appreciated the humor but didn't have it in him to laugh. He stopped in his tracks. Frozen. He'd seen something moving in the hills. It was motion, without shape or definition, which he caught out of the corner of his eye. "Something is there," he said to Lilith, who turned to look the direction Martin had indicated with a slight nod of the head.

He didn't want to look directly. He almost didn't want to know what he'd seen. He wanted to be caught off-guard even less. Lilith sniffed the air and shook her head. "All I can smell is the river."

"Whatever it is, it's hiding. Do you think it's afraid of us?"

"Could be. Could also be an ambush."

"You know, you aren't helping." Martin kept walking. "Still the land of the dead?"

"One of them," Lilith said. "There are a lot of them. Some are like this. Some are battlefields. Some are feasting halls. Others are palaces. A lot of them look like these, though."

"So whatever is watching us is probably . . . dead?"

"It's possible, maybe probable. It could also be things that go between—intermediaries like felines."

"And ravens," Martin smirked and Lilith spat. "There are other things? Other intermediaries?"

"Most certainly."

The sound of stamping feet came rolling towards them over the hills. It wasn't thunderous. It didn't shake the ground, but it demanded attention. Martin was sure whatever it was was getting louder and growing closer. He picked up his pace. With the river on one side, the only place to go was toward the sound or across the water if it came to that.

A couple minutes later, the sound having followed them, Lilith spotted a structure on the banks of the river. "A dock!" She called back to Martin and she picked up her pace, looking over her shoulder to make sure Martin had done the same.

He saw it. He wasn't sure he'd have classified it as a dock exactly. It was a loosely lashed-together collection of planks and driftwood that bobbed with the flow of the dark water. It stretched maybe a dozen feet out and was maybe a foot or so wider than Martin was from shoulder to shoulder. As they got closer, and the dock came better into focus, Martin had hoped they'd see it was sturdier than it first appeared. It did not. He could see that the collection of planks and driftwood was not just a dock, but also a raft, tied to a rotting post stuck in the mud of the eroding bank.

The sound materialized as two horses—both palomino, Martin thought the word was—burst over the top of a hill and were headed towards him and Lilith. A colony of bats appeared overhead from the same direction, back towards the west. More horses appeared on the hills, at a full run, heading in their direction and closer than Martin was comfortable with. He ran and Lilith did the same. Black water and bobbing debris or not, he decided he'd rather be on the water than in the path of those horses.

They were less than fifty yards from the boat launch, or the dock, or whatever the sad structure was meant to be, Martin breathless, cold vapor pouring from his nose and mouth when the rider appeared.

"Hurry!" Martin tried to find more speed. He was stumbling, clambering to find his footing on the uneven bank.

Lilith reached the dock first but did not step onto it.

Martin knew the cat had reacted instinctively to the proximity of the water. "I'll get the raft untied, then you can fit inside my coat. Do you see an oar?"

There was an oar, or rather a long, smoothed branch with one flat end laying a few paces further up the bank.

"Yes. Over here," Lilith ran to the oar and circled it. Martin dashed towards it, picked it up and turned around toward the dock. There were a half dozen horses now, palomino, chestnut, even an all-white one with a blonde mane dancing in the wind it generated charging toward them. Martin wasn't sure if the horses were running toward him or away from the rider.

The rider's horse was an enormous beast, so black it was as though the rider was astride the night itself. It barreled towards Martin and Lilith, the rider leaning forward in the saddle. He was infinitely more terrifying than any costume idea Martin had thought up. The figure was tall and stocky, broad across the shoulders. He wore dark brown pants that stretched to his calves where they met black boots with silver tips. His shirt was white and half hidden beneath the shoulders of the black and crimson cloak that blew around and behind him as he ran.

The head, though—the head was the stuff of nightmares. Martin knew the legend. He'd read the Washington Irving story. He'd seen a couple of movies. The headless horseman had even made its way to the small screen. None of it prepared him for the sight before him. A great pumpkin, twice the size or more of a normal human head, seemed to float a few inches above his shoulders. The face in it was all angles and crooked lines. It was a sneer and a sinister smile at the same time, and flames roared from the mouth, the eyes, and the nose.

The rider said nothing, didn't shout, didn't call out to Martin or Lilith. He simply charged forward on the horse the color of pitch. Martin shook himself loose of the hold the vision had on him and returned to the dock. He set the paddle down, nearly losing it over the side, and fumbled with the rope. It was stiff and cold and he couldn't find purchase with his fingernails to work a bit of it loose. The horses' hoofbeats grew louder. The rider drew closer. Lilith paced at the edge of the violently swaying structure.

Martin groaned. He had only one hand to use. The other held the lantern firmly, its little light dancing wildly making the knot swim in and out of shadow. He dashed to the bank and set the lantern down. Lilith stood guard beside it. Martin returned to the knot, both hands frantically picking at loose ends. Finally, he worked enough of it free to gain some slack and held tight as the raft was loosed from its mooring. One-handed again, straining against the pull of the river, he took the few steps back to the bank, picked up the lantern, and held open his jacket for Lilith to climb in. The elastic waist of the coat created a suitable hammock for her.

With one hand holding the rope and the other the turnip lantern, he had no hands left to take up the oar. He gave it a little kick and it clattered onto the craft. He crawled out after it and released the rope. As they drifted out into the river, the horses ran by, shaking the ground, with the rider in their wake. Martin and Lilith were a third of the way across, Martin fighting with the oar so they wouldn't simply be carried away to who-knew-where further down.

The rider pulled up short of the bank. Martin looked over his shoulder in time to see the rider lift the flaming jack-o'-lantern from his shoulders and hurl it towards them.

* * *

The pumpkin head hit with a splash, casting oily water into the air and down onto Martin and his little craft. He let out a yelp and wiped the cold, wet, slimy-feeling water from his face. No sooner had he wiped it away than a new horror erupted. The flaming heart of the pumpkin had not immediately been doused, rather it had lit a greasy slick in the water and a floating blaze was roaring to life around them.

Martin was not embarrassed by the tears streaming down his face. If ever there was a time for tears, this was it. He tucked his chin into the opening in his coat and said, "The river is on fire!" Lilith hadn't seen the blaze begin—not wanting to poke her head out of Martin's jacket while they were on the water.

"Put the lantern in here with me. I'll keep it upright. You need to row. Fast," she said.

"It will light my coat on fire!"

"I don't think it will. Here." Lilith repositioned so she could curl herself around it. "Now row."

Martin gripped the oar with both hands, kneeling on the little raft, and paddled. He'd never done it before. He'd seen it done on TV and had an idea what it should look like. First one side, then the other. One side, then the other. There was no grace in his technique, clumsily swapping the oar from one side of his body to the other, but he had no time to worry about improving his method. He needed to get across the water. The river was speeding up, and as one little patch of flame flickered out, a new one danced to life. Martin couldn't help but wonder, if they grew close enough, would they light his little raft?

He stroked and stroked, making more progress down river than across. He spared a few glances over his shoulder to keep an eye on the rider who now sat on his mount watching them, a council of shadows and inhuman shapes around him. The rider had a new jack-o'-lantern atop his shoulders. Whether it had grown, reappeared, or if these spirits—or whatever they were—had brought one to him, Martin did not know, nor did he want to.

Eventually the raft reached the opposite bank. Martin's arms were burning. He was soaked and shivering, but they had crossed. The problem now was where to land the raft. There was no dock on this side, or if there was, they had probably passed it. In the shallows, the water moved slower and Martin was able to control the craft's direction a little better. He saw his mark and prepared. "Lilith? Do we need to return to my world from the same place?"

"Not at all. Why?"

"Because we're going to lose this raft. I'm going to lift you out of my coat and when I say jump, I want you to jump as far forward as you can. I'll grab the lantern. Ready?"

"Martin, what are you—?"

"Jump!"

Martin had Lilith under her front legs and propelled her forward as she used her back legs to shove off from Martin's mid-section. He caught the lantern as it tumbled and held it tight. Lilith flew through the air and landed on a muddy, debris-covered section of the bank, a little peninsula that jutted out in the water. It was little more than a collection of branches and brush that had refused to be washed away.

The raft crashed into it with enough force to split it asunder. It had barely been seaworthy to begin with. Martin threw his weight forwards and aimed for solid ground. He landed, holding the lantern to his chest. He gasped for a breath and one leg slipped into the river before he could rearrange his weight and roll to safety.

"Lilith," he called.

"Safe," she said and walked out to him. She licked his cheek and rubbed her face against his, purring.

"I'm okay. I'm okay." He sat up and did an inventory of his body to verify this was the truth. Everything seemed to be working. The lantern was lit and, though the outside of his backpack was pretty soaked, its contents remained dry.

"I need to change. I'm freezing." Martin almost couldn't believe he'd thought to bring extra socks and pants. He had thought it extremely unlikely he'd need them. His mother would have been proud. As he sat on a patch of brown grass, a few feet up from the river bank, enjoying the feel of dry clothes, he couldn't help thinking of his parents. Surely they knew he was gone by now, and they would almost certainly know where he'd disappeared to. They would be upset, not mad maybe, but they'd be in a state, and he felt guilty. But he'd also had no choice.

Lilith lay stretched out beside him, cleaning herself. Martin could feel the relief rolling off her that they were no longer on the water. The last of the flames had died away and the rider and his conspirators had dispersed. "Now what?" she asked. "He knows you're here."

"He might not know where we're going, though."

"He has eyes and ears everywhere, Martin. That has to be how he found you this time."

"The horses?"

"Probably not. Horses are a bit like cats and ravens. The Japanese know them as intermediaries with the Kami, the spirits of one of their worlds."

"Does the rider rule them?"

"I don't think so. I think they were running from him."

Breaths were coming easier now and his heart was no longer pounding loudly in his ears, so Martin rose to his feet and said, "We better keep moving."

Lilith stood, stretched, and agreed.

"East to the stones," Martin said, rubbing his temples.

"North to the village."

"I don't suppose you know what either of those things mean, do you?"

"I know what stones and villages are, but not these. I'm hoping it will be obvious when we've reached them ."

They turned their backs to the river and headed east through a field of wilted wildflowers.

Chapter 28

Mom had suggested they call the police. Dad felt calling the police when they knew where their son was would only tax the city's resources and, worse, draw attention.

"But what if he hasn't crossed yet? What if he's still out there somewhere, lost in the woods? Or maybe he came back, but he's hurt?"

Dad rubbed his face with both hands. These were possibilities. He knew that, and he considered. "Okay. We'll call the police. We'll tell them he was with us when he went to bed last night and that he was gone this morning. They'll ask us about what we were doing. They'll probably want to talk to us separately. Then they'll want to . . . They'll check his laptop and they will see the message he sent Sidney about leaving. Hell, they might read it as a suicide note: 'I'm going to the other side.'"

"But they will see the older messages, too, the ones where they talk about what was going on."

"Yeah, and they'll think drugs or a cult, or god only knows what!" Dad threw his hands in the air. They were standing on the porch trying to decide whether to get in the car and drive around the neighborhood or to the police station. They had been standing there for several minutes, shouting, though not at each other.

Dad turned to Mom and said, "Maybe we call the police, but not yet. We have to think this through. We don't want them to think he's a troubled runaway or that we've driven him off or anything."

Mom was about to reply but was interrupted by a strange, new voice. "I felt something, Mr. and Mrs. Kelly. I felt it last night. I think we all know where young Martin is."

Mom and Dad turned to face the source of the voice. Mom gave a little gasp and stepped back a few feet. Dad shook his head and actually laughed. Neither of them would have believed their eyes or ears had they not had a conversation with a cat and raven in their dining room the night before.

"I'm sorry to startle, folks, but I just couldn't work out how to introduce myself otherwise."

"For the love of sasquatch!" Dad said. "You're not . . ."

"Baxter. Yes, I am; friend of Sidney's. She let me in on what was going on with your son, and I've been staying around to see if I could help. He's a good boy."

"You've met him?" Mom asked.

"I have."

Dad asked, "When?"

Baxter replied, "Maine," and left it at that. Martin's parents did, too—for the time being. Then Mom asked, "What are you doing here this morning? You said you felt something?"

"Yes ma'am. I did. I don't know exactly what it was, but knowing what Martin has been dealing with, I thought it must have something to do with him. Given the bits of conversation I just heard between ya'll, I'm guessing my hunch was right."

Mom and Dad both nodded.

"So, he's filled you in then?" the reindeer asked.

"I think so. You're new to the story, though, so maybe we're not as filled in as we thought," Dad said.

"I helped him sneak off to meet someone we thought could help the night you stayed in South Portland. I apologize for the sneaking around. I have little ones of my own and I would not be best pleased learning another adult had helped them get out from under me, but Martin insisted it wasn't the right time to bring you in and we had only the one lead."

Mom bit her lip. "As a mother—"

But Dad interrupted. "Honey, I know. Maybe we can get into that later. I think we need to find out what Baxter knows so we know how best to proceed."

Baxter bowed her head. "I don't know much. I haven't talked to the boy since Maine. I've been listening. I've been wandering, but I haven't come across anything that would help him directly. What's happened since? When did he leave?"

Dad sat on the top step, bringing him nearly eye level with the reindeer. Mom headed for the kitchen door. "Honey, I'll get some coffee." Then she turned to Baxter, "Do you want . . . anything?"

"If you have hot chocolate, I'd love some. If you don't, or if it would be any trouble, don't you fuss."

"Right," Mom said, and went into the house.

* * *

Gump sat on the dirt floor of the barn where the unlikely fellowship had met previously. He was surrounded by teetering piles of pumpkins, the floor littered with the slimy seeds and guts from their insides. It was the smell of these pumpkin innards which had attracted a certain reindeer who'd been anxiously pacing the surrounding area—trying to remain unseen as she racked her brain over how she could possibly help Martin.

Baxter poked her head in through a hole in one wall of the barn. She swung her great thick neck from side to side, sniffing the unfamiliar aroma. Caught off guard—so focused was he on carving a toothy grin into one of the gourds—Gump startled and leaped to his feet when the reindeer said, "Afternoon."

He could have run. There were several broken places in the walls of the barn he could have slipped between. He could have hidden, putting a tower of pumpkins between himself and the antlered beast who'd snuck up on him. Instead, Gump stood motionless, mouth agape, staring at Baxter.

"Sorry, hon. I didn't mean to startle. That's an awful lot of pumpkins you've got there."

Gump stammered, shuffled his feet. "Lot of them. Yep. All pumpkins now. Jack-o'-lanterns later."

"I see." Baxter bobbed her head. "And you're carving them all yourself?"

The goblin sighed, then pursed his lips together resolutely and nodded his head.

"Whatcha doin' with them all?"

"Pranks. Pranks and tricks. Tricks and treats. Pumpkins shine on Halloween. No one expects them sooner. No one expects them to pop up every old place. If you didn't carve one, you don't expect to have one."

"No. I suppose that's true. That's a fun little trick. I have a good friend who does things like that at Christmas."

"Not for fun. Helping. I have friends helping with tricks. I'm helping friends with tricks."

It can't be a coincidence, Baxter thought. *Jack-o'-lanterns and tricks—lots of them—to help someone in Martin's own neighborhood?*

"When you say helping friends . . . Are you helping Martin?"

"And Jack. And Charlie. And Lilith. She's a cat."

"My name is Baxter. Martin is a friend of mine, too. It's nice to meet you."

"I'm Gump."

"A pleasure, Gump. This here is a mighty fine idea."

"Wish I could do more. Wish I could spread these everywhere. I can't cut fast enough. I can't scoop fast enough. I can't sneak them out as far as I want, but I'll do every bit I can to help until I can think of more."

Baxter grinned. She bobbed her head and said, "Sugah, you keep working. I've got an idea."

Chapter 29

The riverbank had been steep and it had taken Martin three attempts—slipping on mud and loose rock—to climb to the top of the rise. Wet and muddy, he stood and surveyed the land. In the distance was the dark silhouette of mountains. Nearer to them, but still far enough away it seemed an impossible distance after their ordeal on the river, Lilith spotted their next destination.

Martin sighed, relieved. His greatest fear, besides not being able to return to his world, was that they would get lost—had gotten lost when the raft was carried down the river—but there were the rocks the raven had mentioned, and it meant they were back on course.

The rocks, it turned out, couldn't be missed. Many of them were twice or more the size of an average man. Some would have been far larger still were they not broken—fallen into shapeless heaps. They seemed to serve no obvious purpose. They weren't part of a greater structure Martin could see. He wondered if perhaps they had once been like Stonehenge or bore carved faces like the moai of Easter Island. Now they were rubble. They were also a landmark.

"How far have we walked," Martin asked.

"From the river? Farther than I've ever wanted to," Lilith said.

"How long do you think it's been since we crossed over?"

"Well, time works differently here. For us, it's been . . . maybe a day and a half."

"And at home?"

"No way to tell—especially because I think we've been in more than one realm on this side, and for all I know each one has its own clock, so to speak.

It could be just a day and a half on your side as well. It could be much longer."

Color drained from Martin's face. "My parents—"

"It isn't Halloween yet, though. We would know."

Martin asked no more questions. Instead, he focused on the directions.

North to the village. The village came with its own set of questions. Was it occupied or was it like the church? If it was occupied, who with? Or what? What would he and Lilith do once they got there? He hoped another messenger would meet them, one that didn't need convincing to act as a guide.

Martin couldn't help but wonder if it had been the raven from church who had given them up. He had seen birds wheeling overhead since they'd left the river. Some of them, at least, had to be watching him and Lilith. There were other things that had been watching them, too. There was a dramatic ramping up of the number of shadows dancing along the edge of the wood and slipping along the ground where there was nothing there to cast a shadow.

"Martin, this has become a lot more dangerous, you know."

"I know."

"If the rider is after you, then there will be a lot of other things after you, too."

"Yeah. I thought so."

"And though there are many things you can outrun, there are things you cannot."

"I don't even want to think about what those would be."

"And I won't tell you of the ones I know." She was quiet for a moment, though Martin knew she hadn't reached the end of her thought.

"What else, Lilith? What aren't you saying?"

Without turning around, keeping north as they'd been instructed, she said over her shoulder. "I'm saying we can cross back anytime. We have the lantern—Jack. We can go back to your world and come up with another plan."

"We can't. There isn't another plan and we're already here."

"All I'm saying is that this is going to get harder. We are only going to be in more danger and there would be no shame in going back."

"I'll keep that in mind," though Martin had no intention of leaving unless it was a clear life and death choice. Too much depended on them succeeding.

154

And it was true they only had the one plan. If there was something else to try, if there was anything other than going home—sitting around and talking—he'd be more apt to consider it, but that just wasn't the case.

"You're a brave young man, Martin."

"Thank you."

* * *

The rider had thundered up and down the bank looking for a place to cross, but could see none. He ordered the small force assembled with him to cross. They protested they could not. Some said the rules of their land prohibited them from crossing water without a guide. Others—much more simply—complained they couldn't swim.

The rider raged. Flames erupted from his pumpkin head and he shouted at them. He reminded them of his mission and the boy's intent to foil it. He threatened them with punishments he could not himself deliver, but the force of his words and the pure terror they carried was enough to motivate his audience.

Spirits floated and undead things clambered, walked, or crawled to the river's edge. The more corporeal were drowned or washed away. Some fell—or were ripped—apart as they tried to fly across. Others hurled themselves, as though against an invisible wall at the water's edge, to no avail.

The horseman watched, his rage increasing. A mortal boy—in his world—could not be allowed to escape. He thought, "And none of these can see me bested."

He shouted, "Find me that boy!" And a half a dozen long, thick snakes slithered through the weeds and into the water as a murder of crows appeared overhead.

* * *

There was no clear path north from the stones, at least for the first hour's walk. They simply stayed true and kept watch for signs of one. Late into the second hour, they heard music, joyful-sounding music, and laughter, and though they could not yet pinpoint where it was coming from, all they could hope was that it was coming from the village they were intended to find.

They followed the sounds and a path began to emerge. It was two or three meters across and more of a clearing through overgrown weeds and bramble, but it was the closest thing to a path they had found. The voices became louder.

"That's not English," Martin said. "I can't tell what they're saying."

"It sounds familiar, but I can't place it either. It's got to be the village, though."

It wasn't. It was a party, a celebration of some kind, though it was hard to say what of. Two dozen figures or more gathered in a loose circle around an enormous cauldron suspended over a fire. Something inside bubbled and frothed. From the little rise where Martin and Lilith had hidden themselves, they could not see into the pot, or into the tents that were set up outside the circle of dancing, singing, and drinking figures. Smells rose to meet them, though. Whatever was in the pot had once been an animal because the air carried the fatty, sweet smell of meat. There were spice notes in the air, too. They could have been coming from the pot or the barrels the figures were drinking from, which stood upon long wooden tables.

"What are they?" Martin asked.

"I . . . I don't know . . . they . . ."

"Have you ever seen them before?"

"No. I don't think so—certainly not. I'd remember that."

The figures below them ranged in size and shape, in form and probably in species as far as Martin could tell. Some were about his own size and some taller than the tallest man he'd seen. Some were so thin Martin couldn't see how they could stand erect and some so fat he wasn't sure how they moved. But their sizes were the least remarkable thing about them. These creatures were a hodgepodge of pieces. They were mammal and bird, reptile and insect. Martin wasn't entirely sure there wasn't a stone or plant among them. It was as though someone had mixed a collection of jigsaw puzzle pieces, cast them into piles, and called them finished.

And the creatures had creatures of their own. One rode an alligator, one had a serpent wrapped around it, coiled between legs and arms, and around her neck. One was surrounded by a cloud of black insects.

"Dukes and duchesses!" One of them called, raising a horn full of sloshing drink above his head. This one most resembled a satyr if it resembled anything Martin was familiar with. The crowd quieted.

They called to one another, laughed and shouted. As Martin listened, their words melted from the otherworldly language he'd first heard into understandable English. He looked at Lilith and cocked an eyebrow. She nodded her head and turned her attention back to the gruesome host.

One of their number rose to its feet—a creature who appeared to be assembled mostly of pig and leopard, but sporting a feathered ruff. It raised its drinking horn to above its head and said, "Tonight we celebrate. Tonight we drink! Tonight we feast and make merry, for tomorrow we continue the hunt!"

A great cheer erupted from the crowd and a sweat broke out on Martin's brow. He looked at Lilith again but could not read her reaction.

"The rider has taken more land and more people. Many of the Fae folk—and others—have become refugees. They seek shelter wherever it can be found. They build settlements to keep them safe. But we cannot be kept out!"

Another cheer.

"We cannot be hidden from!"

A louder cheer and the sloshing of more drinking horns.

"Tomorrow, the refugees will run and we, the dukes and duchesses, collect new trophies for our walls and food for our stores."

Lilith slapped at Martin's hand. He looked at her to see that she was slinking backwards, away from the ledge, pressed as close to the ground as she could get. Martin belly-crawled back until he thought it would be safe to stand without being spotted.

"What is going on down there?"

"They're bad, Martin. They are very bad. Before all this—before you met Jack—what's the worst place you could think of in what you knew as the underworld. Don't say it!"

Martin closed his mouth.

"They are from that place. They are the royalty of that place, and they have benefited greatly from the rider. They have been able to gather more souls to their realm than ever."

"You're saying those are—"

"Please. Maybe it's superstitious, but you can't speak it. You can't say their names. Don't name the place. It'll draw their attention."

Martin scratched his head. "They're hunting. They . . . they want to collect souls? And they mentioned settlements and—"

"The village," Lilith said. "I think they are going to sack the village. We have to get there and then get out before they attack."

"Is there any way to stop them?"

"None that I know. Certainly not one that a fourteen-year-old boy and a single cat can manage."

Martin wondered if there was something they could do before setting off for the village; poison their drink, trap them, lead them off the trail, but decided if any of that could be done, he didn't know how. It sounded like video game or cartoon ideas when he really considered it. He found himself wishing very hard at that moment that he lived in a video game or a cartoon.

Chapter 30

He couldn't spare many. It was too close to Christmas—too much for them to do—but if he didn't offer some kind of help, what work they'd done for Christmas might not matter. So, Mr. Claus announced at breakfast one morning that he'd heard from Baxter and that the reindeer had an idea how to help Sidney's friend Martin. Hearing there was a chance to help Sidney had been enough to capture the attention of most of the assembled workers. When he explained the reindeer's idea, the rest of them were rapt.

And so it was that two teams—selected by Emmett from an overwhelming number of volunteers—arrived at a dilapidated barn in Carlisle, Massachusetts, to the alarm and glee of a pudgy goblin.

"Gump, I'm Emmett. I'm a friend of Baxter. She said you needed some help. Here we are."

A platoon of elves had lined the walls of the barn and snapped to attention—carving tools, knives, and wooden scoops held at the ready.

Gump jumped up and down slapping his long-fingered hands together letting out little squeaks.

"Two teams," Emmett continued. "This is the carving team. Let them know what you need and they'll get started. This isn't something they've done before, but they're excited to try it. They work really well as an assembly line—years of practice."

"Ooh!" Gump said. "Not assembling. Cut out the tops. Scoop. Cut a face. Spooky faces. Scary face. Not cute faces. You're elves. No cute elf faces. Monster. Demons. Witches. Ghosts," He paused a moment, then added, "Goblin faces," and laughed at his joke until tears ran down his eyes.

The carving team arranged themselves into a production line as the goblin guffawed. Emmett waited for Gump to catch his breath, then said, "Team two is the delivery team—many of them Baxter's family—they'll take care of bringing you more pumpkins. Then, whatever we have finished, they will deliver as far and wide as we need them to. I'll coordinate from up north."

"Thank you, Emmett the elf. Martin and Lilith and Jack and Charlie—they thank you too."

Emmett reached out a hand to shake.

"Spider." Gump said with a scowl. He smacked the wrist of Emmett's coat, then shook the elf's hand.

* * *

It wasn't like the church at all. That was the first thing that struck him. The buildings were whole. They might not have been in the greatest of shape, not the kinds of things you'd see on a travel brochure, but they had all their walls and appeared to have all their roofs. There were windows—not with glass panes, just open spaces that could be covered with shutters, and most of these shutters were both open and intact. It was not at all what Martin had expected, and he was glad of that.

Far stranger, compared to what they'd seen so far, was the place appeared populated. As he and Lilith approached they had seen people in the streets—just a few but clearly there, if not entirely corporeal. As they came closer, they could hear what almost sounded like the normal goings on of life in an old, quiet town. Martin was not a student of early Anglo-Saxon architecture, or he might have thought the village looked northern European and around four hundred years old. Lilith might have thought it. Neither of them mentioned it.

"Just because it looks normal, doesn't mean those spirits are friendly," Lilith said.

"We can't assume they aren't, though."

"Sure we can. I tend to assume everything is unfriendly until I have reason to think it's not."

She had suggested they keep off the road and approach from the underbrush or between buildings, taking reconnaissance until they knew what they were dealing with. She'd not even finished explaining her very feline plan before she was already slinking and skulking. Martin disregarded the plan and took the direct route.

Not only was this the village they were supposed to find, he thought, but the unsuspecting spirits dwelling there were right in the path of the hunting demons. Whether they could help him or not, *he* could try to help *them*. Either they took his warning and it earned him a return favor or they didn't listen to him and maybe ripped him limb from limb. He wouldn't know until he tried, and he needed to hold on to some hope.

Martin strolled down the wide, dusty lane that was clearly the main thoroughfare through the town. He walked right down the middle, looking for all the world like he belonged there. He looked into windows, top and bottom floors, and tried to spy one of the spirits he knew was about.

Throwing all caution to the wind and hoping against all odds it wasn't the worst possible thing he could do, Martin called out, "Hello! I don't know who can hear me, but I have news I think you want to hear."

No one answered. At least, no one said anything. A few spirits did emerge from shops along the path. The shops had no wares visible, but Martin knew them for what they were by the kinds of display cases in the windows. A spirit who had once been a heavy man came through the door of what he imagined was supposed to look like a bakery. Maybe it had once been a bakery, in another world. Maybe it still was a bakery in that world. A woman emerged from what would have been a butcher's, and two others from what was either a home or an office of some kind. There wasn't enough detail to tell.

As soon as they emerged, Martin went on. "Thank you for listening. I am searching for something and was led to this village. On the way, in fact, just a couple of hours ago—I think—I came across a hunting party." The spirits looked from one to another. A few more faces had appeared in windows and looked at the boy intently.

"They called themselves dukes and duchesses. I'm not really sure what that means, but they seemed pretty proud of it. They also seemed pretty interesting in hunting souls. I think they are headed this way."

A slender spirit, what had once been a lanky man with sharp features and well-tailored clothes, floated towards Martin and asked, "Were they with the rider?"

"No. They said the rider made things easier for them. They said something about refugees."

"How did you escape their notice?" A woman with a tight bun atop her head asked from the side of the road.

"I don't know. I think I did, though. They didn't attack, at least."

"And why would you warn us?" The first man asked. "You aren't one of us."

"I'm not, but I know bad people . . . er, things, when I see them and I guess I figured if they're bad then maybe it would be a good thing to warn whoever they are after."

The slender spirit rested his hands on his hips and laughed, a smile turning up the corners of his mouth. He was joined by a handful of other spirits, who he turned to and said, "We have before us a mortal boy who has crossed the veil to save our small community from being savaged by the royalty of Hades itself!"

The gathered crowd laughed and cheered. Some sneered, skeptical and uncomfortable. Martin said, "To tell the truth, I came looking for something. I was told to come here. I don't know if what I'm looking for is here, but this was the next step in my directions."

"And what is it you are looking for?" One of the spirits asked.

"A . . . talisman. An artifact charged with the power the rider is gathering." The spirits' faces changed, mostly in surprise or in fear. "No! No, I don't work for him. I am trying to get this item back to the other side, to shift the balance and take back some of his power."

If spirits drew breath, at this time they allowed a collective sigh. There was still suspicion on some of their faces, but they seemed mostly put at ease.

The slender man said, "I know of no such artifact here, my boy. We are but a humble burg of forgotten souls."

There were general nods and quiet sounds of agreement. Martin lowered his head a little.

"Oh, no!" The spirit continued, "We're happy to be forgotten. No one is looking for us. No one is trying to bring us under heel. As long as we are forgotten, we are not a bother to anyone and no one is a bother to us . . . unless of course we are hunted by the foulest beasts. Thank you for the warning, by the way. I'm afraid I don't think there's anything here that can help you, though."

Martin knew that was a possibility. This village could very well be just the next stop in a long series of waypoints guiding them towards the quill they sought. After the woods, the clearing, the hills, and the river, though, Martin needed a rest. Whatever the village was good for, it seemed a safe enough place to catch their breath.

Lilith sauntered up to Martin and weaved in and out between his ankles. Martin faced the spirits and said, "I'm Martin, by the way. This is Lilith. We're together." Lilith let out a slight meow.

A pot-bellied spirit with what had once been miles of curly hair directed Martin and Lilith to a building that seemed to suggest a pub. There wasn't anything to eat, nor anything to drink, but it had small tables, stools at a bar, and a wide hearth. Martin sat at a stool at the bar and placed the lantern, happily flickering down beside him. The jovial spirit indicated that he'd like to stay and chat, but the villagers were meeting outside to decide what to do about the hunting party. He said they were welcome to join him, but assumed they'd want a rest first.

The spirit wandered out through the door they'd come in and vanished from sight. Martin drew in a long, slow breath and let it out again. His feet were sore. His head hurt. His throat was dry and swollen. This village was a welcome respite. It recharged him a bit to find something so normal, but he couldn't help but think he was still a long way from getting where he needed to go.

Then there was a scratching noise from the corner of the room. A spirit sat at a table in a shadowed alcove, scratching at a bit of paper with an old quill. Martin's heart leapt. Lilith went into a crouch, prepared to leap for the feather and run for it. The spirit looked up from his work and said, "I might know where you need to go next."

Chapter 31

"Not far from here, I couldn't tell you exactly, but near enough to walk there and back in an afternoon, there's a cave. It's not very deep. You can still see a little light coming in, even when you've reached the very bottom. I found it just out wanderin'."

"What's in the cave, sir?" Martin asked.

"Well, I couldn't tell you for sure what's there. It's an odd little place. There are some shelves along the wall of the chamber at the far end. Tall shelves, kind of narrow. I suppose they look like bookshelves, but I don't recall seeing any books on them. They aren't full."

"And why," Lilith asked, "do you suppose it's what we're looking for?"

"I can't say for certain. I know objects from the other side when I see 'em, though. There aren't that many things that make their way over here. Most spirits probably go their eternity without ever coming across one. This place had a few of 'em."

Hearing this, Martin had to stop himself from running out the door immediately. He didn't want to be rude, but more importantly, he realized, he didn't know which direction he should run in.

Lilith, sensing his urgency, said, "That is intriguing, and promising. I must say. Any idea what sort of place the cave is? What's it doing there, and what or who has collected these strange things?"

The spirit sat upright in his chair and appeared to lean back a little. "I've wondered about that. Seems strange. Then again, this land is strange and gets stranger all the time. I suppose someone was hiding them or trying to keep them safe, or both. I tell you how to get there yet?"

"No, sir," said Martin. "You just mentioned it wasn't far."

"No, it isn't. I was out wanderin' that day—I think I mentioned. So, I couldn't tell precisely and I've only found my way back there maybe once."

Martin could feel his heart slide into his stomach.

"But," the spirit continued, "you've got to head to higher ground for sure. There wouldn't be a cave here in the lowlands, least I don't think there would be. I suppose I don't know how that works, certainly not here I don't. But it starts to get rocky. You don't have to go as far as the ice. It gets cold quickly that way. It's before the ice."

"Is there a path?" Martin asked.

"Not as such. No. Maybe if you were a tracker you might see the land differently, but I didn't follow one. I'll bet you're a bit of a tracker though, aren't you?" he said looking at Lilith.

"Mostly mice and small birds, but I have a sense of things."

"A sense of things . . ." the spirit repeated. "Maybe without a map or directions that's how a person finds a thing."

"Sir," Martin said, "wupe appreciate the help. I think you're right. This sounds like the sort of thing we need to have a look at. Can you remember anything else?"

The spirit interlaced his fingers across his ample belly and appeared to consider. He scratched at his chin and he seemed to be looking up and to the left like he was searching for a clue in his memory that might or might not be there. "You can't see the moon," he said.

"Pardon?" Lilith asked.

"I hadn't thought about that 'til just now, but as I'm looking at the place in my mind's eye it seems to me that you couldn't see the moon."

Martin's first thought was that naturally you couldn't see the moon from inside a cave, but he kept this to himself, hoping there was more to it. "Was it hidden behind something?"

"Could have been," the spirit said and seemed to still be seeing the place in his mind.

Lilith asked him, "Why aren't you with the rest of the townsfolk, planning?"

"I'm no good at planning. Wandering, writing things down, thinking, those are my specialties. In life I was awfully good at eating too," he said with a chuckle. "I'll let them plan and decide and coordinate. Then I'll do what they tell me to do."

"Well, I think we're going to rest our feet a little here if you don't mind. Then we need to find this cave. If you think of anything else, please let us know."

"I will." He lifted his quill from the table, touched the tip of it to his tongue, then dunked it in an inkwell Martin couldn't see. Maybe it wasn't even there. He and Lilith returned to the stools they had occupied, in silence. Martin still wanted to go running off, but knew it wasn't the right approach. He needed to think.

* * *

When Martin was in the second grade, eight years old, his family had taken a trip to Washington, D.C. They had visited the Smithsonian Air and Space Museum, the National Archives, and walked a trail taking in most of the major monuments. All of those things were vivid and happy memories Martin carried with him, but there was one memory from the trip that stood out in the greatest detail. He carried it with him, but it didn't come up as a happy feeling. It came up as hairs standing up on the back of his neck. He and his parents chuckled a little about it now when they'd get to "remember the time" around a dinner table with extended family, but at the time there had been nothing funny about it at all.

They had taken the morning on the second to last day of their trip to visit the National Zoo. The weather had kept them away the first few days, but the forecast had been clear that morning. Martin marveled at the big cats, was fascinated by the antics of the primates, and waited anxiously to see the panda cubs come out from hiding behind their rotund mother.

The weather changed in a flash. The sky darkened in a matter of seconds, and there was a clap of thunder that felt like it shook the walkways beneath their feet. The thunder was unnerving enough, but the roars, squeals, shouts, trumpets, and whines of the whole menagerie was—to that day—the worst cacophony Martin had ever heard. Zookeepers rushed to open doors for indoor enclosures and usher animals inside. It only lasted a minute, but it was a minute of unholy orchestra.

And right now, that same orchestra began screaming in the near distance and getting closer quickly. "The demons!" Lilith said, jumping off her stool. "Hear them?"

"Oh, god yeah. What do we do?"

"Run," the spirit in the corner said. "You could stay, I suppose, but there's nothing on the menu and the taps are dry. I believe I'll take my leave." He seemed to dissolve into the air.

Martin heard the laments of the other spirits in the village then. They had heard the beasts, too. He hoped whatever plan they had come up with would keep them out of the clutches of those awful beasts. He knew it couldn't be as simple as vanishing as the stranger in the corner had. These creatures hunted souls and sounded like they were quite confident in their ability to do so.

All this ran through Martin's mind as he ran after Lilith through the door. "Which direction?" he called.

"This way," Lilith replied, and ran down a narrow path between two of the buildings that lined the little main street. As he ran, Martin could see the residents of the hamlet, appearing and disappearing, running or floating this way and that. He saw a dozen or more of them had simply taken off down the main avenue and were headed quickly away from town.

No idea how she'd chosen their direction, Martin assumed Lilith knew what she was doing and hurried after her. In only a couple hundred yards it began to feel like the right idea. The land started to slope upwards again and the trail they were blazing through the hills was becoming more sparse and rocky.

Behind them, howling laughter and shouting merged with what had to be the sounds of buildings being demolished or at least substantially damaged. The dukes and duchesses were not subtle hunters. They had no feline stealth, at least not the ones they could hear—but Martin remembered they had come in a twisted variety of shapes, sizes, and assembled pieces.

The wind was picking up and it was a chill and unwelcome addition to the arduous task of running for their lives. The way was becoming uneven, and the hills rolling more sharply. At the crest of one, they saw they were no longer in what could be described as the foothills, and had actually made it into the mountains. Out of the charcoal sky the silhouette of three great peaks had emerged, the peaks reflecting the sickly yellowish hue of the moon.

Chapter 32

All they knew was they didn't want to go far enough into the mountains to reach ice, though the temperature had dropped so quickly Martin didn't think they'd need to go much higher for that to happen.

"We don't even know which way to go! Tell me you've got a map with the big red X to mark the spot," he tried to yell to Lilith, but it came out as a kind of wheeze.

The cat slowed to a walk and Martin did the same. She said, "We only know it's less than half a day's walk for a wandering spirit. ."

"And it's before it gets icy. How far is half a day's wander for a ghost?" Martin asked rhetorically."

"And you can't see the moon," Lilith added.

Martin looked to the sky. The moon was perfectly clear from where they were standing. He ran his gaze along the horizon, towards the mountain peaks. He couldn't work out at what angle they might hide the moon, if they did at all. And that would depend on both direction and time of day.

The roars and screams from the village were still audible, but distant enough, Martin felt comfortable slowing their pace. A thought struck him an almost physical blow, "Lilith, what if it's a trap?"

Her ears perked.

"I mean, what if that ghost sent us up here to get lost? How do we know he doesn't answer to the rider? The raven in the church . . ."

"He could have sent us on to the village for an ambush or to meet someone who would lay the trap, but that seems a little elaborate. We weren't ambushed and we did warn the villagers . . ."

"So maybe it's not a trap?" Martin said, rubbing his face with both hands. He still wasn't sure. "But it might as well have been. I mean, what are we supposed to do, roam the mountain until we starve, freeze to death, or stumble into this cave?"

"As I said once before, we could—"

"No! We can't go back. Not now. Not after we've come this far. You can go back if you have to, but I'm staying."

As if to punctuate the point, Martin held the lantern out before him and slowly turned a full circle, looking for a clue. Lilith sighed, a sound Martin hadn't heard before. He'd heard his grandma's dog sigh when it made itself comfortable in the corner of the couch, but never a cat. She wandered around at the edge of the lantern's little pool of light.

"I could scout ahead a bit. I hate to leave you alone, but as long as you have the lantern and stay put, I can find my way back to you."

They had talked about this strategy in the woods, when they had first arrived, but Lilith had sensed Martin wasn't prepared to be left on his own. Then they had been in the clearing and racing along the river, so there really hadn't been anywhere for her to scout.

"I don't want to sit in one place and wait," he said. "I should keep looking too, but I guess it makes sense if you search a little ahead and then come back."

"Right. Then I can head in another direction. We can cover a lot of ground that way. I can see just fine, and you have old Jack in the lantern."

The little coal sputtered in the turnip. It occurred to Martin that he'd almost forgotten Jack was in there. He'd clutched the lantern for dear life since they had crossed the veil, but after the candles in the church it had mostly been just a lantern. If the spirits in the village had noticed that he carried a spirit around with him, trapped in the coal, they hadn't said anything. They hadn't reacted at all.

He turned the open face of the lantern toward him and before his face. "Jack, you still in there?" The coal brightened briefly "I don't suppose you have underworld GPS capability do you?" Nothing happened.

"I didn't think so."

171

"I wonder if he can sense things from the other side, though—from your side . . . uh, our side."

"What do you mean?"

"I mean, that spirit in the village said things from the other side were rare. I'm sure you stand out like a beacon, but maybe other things do, too. Maybe the artifacts give off a . . . I don't know."

The lantern flared a little. "Do they?" Martin asked it. Nothing happened.

"Okay, so . . . I do think there's something to it," Lilith posited. "But maybe it's not a . . . trail or a vibration or . . . Martin! Maybe it's not everything from the other side; maybe it's things from that side full of Jack-o'-Lightning!"

The coal brightened enough the little pool of light extended a foot or so and remained that way for several seconds.

"Maybe he can sense, maybe all spirits can sense, powerful things of either side, at least if they are looking or paying attention." Now the lantern pulsed. It did so for only a few more seconds, then went almost dark.

"Jack?" There was a slight flicker. "Did you use up too much juice? I didn't think that could happen on this side." The light stayed steady. Martin looked uneasily at Lilith, who shook her head.

"We stick to the plan for now?" she asked.

"Pick a direction," Martin said and they started walking again.

Chapter 33

The rider wasn't the most powerful force in the worlds beyond the veil. He wasn't the first to set his sights on domination. He was only the latest. In a vast conglomeration of disparate worlds, each with its own rules, structures, power hierarchies, legends, and in some cases pantheons, a lone headless rider was far from the greatest force. He knew this. And there were places he didn't tread, places he turned a blind eye to so those who feared him wouldn't see that he had fears of his own.

He had learned to wield fear though, his own and the ambient energy of it around him. Once he'd grown confident in his ability to use fear to influence and control others, he'd begun his conquest.

The rider was of a singular vision. He was once a man, living a normal if not entirely moral life relative to the standards of his day. He'd been punished, cursed—wrongly he would tell anyone who would listen—and had been forced to take the mantle of the rider. His mortal life was ended and his days as a symbol of fear, as a bedtime story, as a warning about staying on the righteous path went on until the mortal world had no use for him. He'd been called across the veil. The man he'd once been, buried deep inside the avatar he'd become, had held out hope that he would return to being just a man, even if only in the realm of the dead. He would be the master of his own life again.

When this didn't happen, when he had to accept that a life had been stolen from him, two things happened. First, a deep and burning hatred for the mortal world took root. It was there that he'd been punished. It was there that people went about their business living lives they had no more right to than he. It was the mortal world where he'd been forced to serve and the mortal world that had forgotten him when the dark wasn't as pitch and the woods not so scary. The second thing was, he decided to embrace his role. He no longer wanted to cast it off and go on existing as a man. He wrapped the role around him like his black and crimson cloak and began, even in the first days beyond the veil, to orchestrate his return to, and punishment of, the mortal world.

There were things he knew to be more powerful, and perhaps even more singular in their drive. Among these things were the royalty of the depths, the demons who called themselves the dukes and duchesses. One, on his or her own, was easily managed or simply avoided. Even two or three, though a challenge, could be worked around. The rider had his own, not friends perhaps, but compatriots. But the whole of Hades's vile clan was well beyond his ability to handle. He couldn't topple them with fear. He couldn't rally enough brave or desperate souls to rise against them, and he certainly couldn't best them in combat.

So, when word reached him that they had gathered and were on the hunt, he knew to stay clear. When news reached him that they were on the hunt in the same region as his own quarry, he knew he could not.

After his encounter with the boy and his cat, the rider had ridden upriver to a bridge in what he thought of as the shattered lands. It had taken hours, perhaps the better part of a day, to make his way there and cross. The boy had a considerable lead on him. And if he was not the interloper's only pursuer, he had to make haste.

He and his mount were in the foothills, approaching the place where the demons had been spotted. As he looked around, getting his bearings and looking for escape routes his prey could have taken, it occurred to him he recognized the place. He wheeled his mount around to face northeast and kicked the horse's flanks. The rider knew what the boy was after, and he couldn't be allowed to reach it.

* * *

It was impossible to tell how much ground they covered. Martin would walk a way and Lilith would run ahead. She'd return, they'd walk a little further and then she would scout. It seemed a sensible way to survey the landscape, but after what had to have been a couple of hours, they'd come no closer to finding a cave. They had paused to have a look around them together, to choose which angle they should take from their current direction, when they heard it.

The sounds from the demons who'd reached the village had mostly subsided. Even from a distance, Martin knew some of them had broken off—presumably chasing souls who'd gotten away from the initial attack. The air had grown almost silent, only the steady wind for a soundtrack.

But the silence was broken. The howls and wails, screeches and squeals rose again—distant, but reinvigorated.

"Perhaps they've found new prey," Lilith said.

"Perhaps that prey is us," Martin replied. They stared at each other, each working out what to say when they heard the chorus again, and this time it was closer.

"Oh, god!" Martin said, "We have to find this cave! Jack? Jack? If you're still in there, point us in the right direction."

The lantern flickered a moment. Martin felt sure it wasn't going to come back to its previous life, but held it up before him and could see that it was growing slightly brighter—slower than it had before—but the change was noticeable if you watched carefully. He held the turnip at arm's length and began to slowly turn in a circle, hoping for some sign. As he turned, the light dimmed. As he continued, it began to brighten again. Martin kept turning and the light grew brighter, then dimmer again as he completed the circuit.

"Turn again. The other way. Go back that way," Lilith insisted.

Martin did. Watching the light very carefully, with the intensity perhaps only a feline can, she said, "Stop," at what seemed to be the point in the circle where the lantern—where Jack—was glowing most brightly."

"That way," Lilith said and they jogged across the increasingly rocky hills.

When the light began to fade again, Martin stopped and repeated the process of turning the lantern around him and was able to make a slight course correction. Filled with hope for the first time in what seemed like forever, Martin's pace was quick and light. Several times he had to stop and turn a bit, not noticing the light had dimmed again in his haste. They had a direction and their goal was close. He could feel it and he thought Lilith could feel it too.

He thought he could also feel the rumble of approaching beasts through the soles of his feet.

* * *

Progress with the novel was steady. Naturally, Dale didn't like everything he'd written, but the act of writing felt far more "right" than he ever supposed it would. He didn't know if it was Jack-o'-Lightning, adrenaline, or perhaps a sense of freedom born from breaking his own rules about the act, but something pulsed within him. Something crackled.

The novel wasn't the only thing he'd made progress with. Dale had been making phone calls—many of his contacts surprised to hear from the renowned recluse—and enticed them to join his efforts to invigorate the Halloween season with fresh tales of terror. The groundwork was being laid. It seemed many people in the scare business shared the opinion that it was time to turn up the volume on fright. "If they only knew," Dale thought. He hadn't explained to anyone about Martin and his mission. That would not have earned him support, he calculated. That would more likely get him labeled as the recluse who'd lost his mind.

Dale was standing on his front porch, cup of tea in hand, breathing in the crisp morning air, enjoying the calm and watching the ravens circle when what at first appeared to be an apocalyptic asteroid headed for Maine resolved itself into a reindeer and came in for a quick landing on his walkway.

Tea spilled, cup fumbled but caught before it crashed to the porch floor, Dale stammered. Baxter shook a little, lifted each of her legs in the air as though to stretch, and took a breath.

"Mr. Connors," she said.

Dale shook his head. "Of course you talk. Why wouldn't you talk?" He walked down the steps and gave Baxter a once over. "I kind of liked the glow stick look on you."

Baxter whickered. "That's a special occasion look, hon. But thank you."

"What are you doing here? Is everything okay? Where's Martin?"

"He's still on the other side. No word has gotten across that I know about. But I am one-hundred percent certain he's going to be coming through right here."

"Here?"

"Yes, sir. You know what he's after, right?"

"Poe's last quill."

"And he ain't going to bring it to show-and-tell. He'll bring it here."

"And you're here . . ."

"In case he needs me."

Chapter 34

The bite in the air was becoming wicked. Martin wanted to stop and put on every layer in his backpack, but knew that some would still be wet and didn't want to take the time. The land was now growing steep quickly and instead of rubble and small boulders, they were encountering craggy spikes and jagged outcroppings of rock that Martin was certain would look like teeth from the right angles.

He and Lilith had become almost certain the horde was hunting them, or at least hunting in their direction and had no idea the kind of pace they could keep, so every rock they passed that didn't reveal a cave felt like more time gone that they couldn't afford to waste. Jack's light had grown steadily brighter and they'd only had to make a few turns against his apparent navigation to work around particularly tall spired or jagged edges.

"We have to be close!" Martin called ahead to Lilith.

"I hope so," she replied over her shoulder.

And then there was the sound of hoofbeats.

Lilith continued to scout ahead as they had been doing previously, only now she could limit the arc of her search to what fell in the direction of Jack's light. She too had heard the hoof beats but hadn't said anything because scaring Martin any further wouldn't serve a purpose. She'd thought at first that the hoof beats must have been made by one of the horde that seemed now to be on their trail, but it had become clear it was a lone rider approaching from a different direction.

"He's coming!" Martin yelled. He stopped, leaned against a black rock spire for a moment to catch his breath, relax the shaking in his legs, and get his bearings. To be certain of his direction before he set out again, he held the lantern before him and began to turn in a circle. As he did, returning almost to the direction in which they had been headed, he noticed something that made his eyes go saucer-like. "Lilith! Lilith, look!"

He pointed to a spot in the near distance where another of the toothy rock formations jutted from the ground. This one was higher, sharper, and more twisted than most they'd seen. The shards of stone crossed one another at points near their tops, having risen at steep angles from the uneven ground below.

"I can't see the moon," he said. He walked several paces to the left and several paces to the right of where he'd been standing, peering at the stones and searching for the moon. It hadn't grown any darker. The sickly yellow light was still nearly enough to see by, but the hill's rocky teeth, up a steep rise from where they stood and framed by a pair of the range's peaks, formed a sort of wall behind which the moon was hidden.

"It's got to be right here. We've got to be right on top of it," Martin was scanning every which way, his head on a swivel.

Lilith made a small circle, searching in the darkness. "I don't see anything yet, Martin," she said. She still hadn't abandoned the idea that it could all be a trap, especially with the sound of the rider approaching.

Martin again rotated the lantern which glowed hotly when faced in a particular direction and they took off at a run.

* * *

The cave was less than a hundred yards further on. The moon was still obscured and the entrance hidden in shadows, but it was there—a narrow slice in the earth—flanked on either side by clusters of jagged stone.

As soon as they stood before the entrance, Jack's light grew very dim. Martin and Lilith fixed each other with a curious glance. "Maybe because we're here . . .?" Martin said.

Hoof beats.

"So he doesn't give us away," Lilith said.

Lilith had no problem with the cave. Her slender frame and feline night vision made it easy to make it down the single curving path to the small chamber at the far end. Martin fit, but barely. Had the passage been any narrower, he'd have had to shimmy sideways. He kept the lantern in front of him and pierced the darkness well enough that he could be sure of his footfalls.

Once he reached the chamber, he set Jack in his lantern down on what appeared to be an antique writing desk. There were no papers, and no quill and ink. It couldn't have been that easy. The chamber was no more than ten feet, maybe twelve in any direction, and was only open a few feet over Martin's head. On one wall was the small desk upon which was a metal stand and circular arm that might once have held a globe. To the left of that was what seemed to be a hat rack, but fashioned out of some material Martin couldn't place. It wasn't anything he'd seen before, and probably native to one of the worlds on this side of the veil. It held no hats, but there was a tattered red scarf hung on one peg-like protuberance.

On the opposite wall were a pair of bookcases. They reached almost to the chamber's stone ceiling, were about two and a half feet wide, and had unevenly spaced shelves. The assortment of objects on them looked like a screen capture from a hidden-objects puzzle game, only more sparse. There was a pair of scissors, a hand mirror, a few pieces of mismatched jewelry, a wooden toy fire truck, a sleigh bell, a leather gun holster, and a couple small wooden boxes.

Having hopped on the desk, Lilith could see the top shelves and relayed that it was more of the same. There were a few coins, the broken hilt of a sword, and a drawing pad whose paper had all gone yellow by the looks of the curled edges.

Neither of them saw the quill. Martin began to move things around on the shelves, kicking up a cloud of dust that made them both sneeze. Lilith jumped from the desk to the second highest shelf and nosed around a bit more. She knocked a few things to the floor, as cats do, but none of them was a feather pen.

"Can you sense anything? Do you smell anything?"

"Just dust. I can't smell anything but dust and mustiness—and something you must have stepped in back there."

Martin scraped his sneakers against the cold stone, then lifted one of the wooden boxes from a lower shelf and set it on the desk. He turned and reached for a second when a sound from the mouth of the cave stopped him.

"Not very bright, closing yourself in a cave like that, boy." The voice was not human. It hissed a little and there was a bit of rumble to the vowels. "You'll either get lost or stuck. Might be that cave is a dead end. What then, child of man?" Martin couldn't tell if this was the same or a different voice from the first. The words buzzed in his ears and made him feel a little light headed.

"Should we come in and rescue you?" This voice was a higher pitch, almost squeaky at the ends of each word, and the laugh that followed was a fork scraping a dinner plate.

Lilith was all bristles and flat ears, arched back and wide eyes. Martin was stunned speechless. Then another sound. This one coming from over their heads, hoof beats. And then a new voice, this one less animal but still not entirely human. "This one is mine," it said, the words only slightly muffled by the rocks.

"Come out, human," one of the demons whispered. It seems there is some contest as to who shall have you. You might have to judge that contest. Of course, we could just come in there and split you into pieces to share."

Then a skittering. Lilith jumped atop the bookshelves and hissed. Martin scanned the path out of the cave and saw dozens, perhaps a hundred scorpions—shiny, black, and nearly the size of his fist. They covered the floor and were moving towards him quickly, tails raised and pincers clicking.

Martin raised one foot to stomp the nearest of them, but realized he'd never get them all. As quickly as they arrived in the cave they stopped. One of the voices from outside of the cave echoed down the rock. "We promise pain if you remain in there, boy. Come out, or be driven out."

Martin was compelled to leave the chamber. Lilith protested. Jack flashed repeatedly from his place inside the lantern, but as Martin saw it, there was no choice. He might die outside the cave. He might have his soul torn from his body or be taken somewhere and tortured. If he remained, he'd starve or freeze. He knew his body wouldn't last as long as his pursuer's patience. Or, they would come in after him and he'd meet the same fate as if he walked outside.

He took a step and the scorpions formed a circle around him, ensuring he could only move in the direction they allowed. "Keep looking," Martin said and was herded out of the cave.

It was game over.

Martin emerged from the cave slowly, calling softly, "I'm coming," as he did.

Chapter 35

At the mouth of the cave, not more than a few dozen feet back was a semicircle, or as close to one as they could make given the terrain, of those horrible beasts they'd seen around their campfire earlier. Up close, they were worse. He could see boils and blisters, sores and dripping wounds. He could smell them. He didn't know if it was horrid breath or their natural perfume, but it was eye-wateringly offensive. He imagined boiled garbage and warm dumpsters. The sound of stomping hooves . . . and turned around. On a small rise, just above the mouth of the cave, sat the rider on his midnight stallion.

"This boy, this human who has found his way to our world through some trickery or foul means—perhaps enslaving a spirit in his lantern—is here to rob me. He means to interfere."

"What care we if he interferes, rider?" A beast with a face like a medieval plague mask asked.

"We take him and it solves your problem of interference."

"I need to know what he knows," the rider said.

"What he knows is of no concern to *us*. It's not his mind we crave."

"I have no quarrel with you. I bear you no ill will nor have I ever come between you and your prey, but I must insist this one is mine. I'll question him and then once I have no more use for him, he's yours to hunt."

"Hand him to us?" one of the creatures hissed. "We do not take captured prey. We hunt. And we have hunted him here."

"Give me time to extract what I need from him, then I will release him for you to hunt as you please."

Several of the beasts seemed to consider. A few were grinding teeth or scratching the stony earth with hooked claws or razor talons. One of these spoke next. "You speak as though you do us a favor, rider. We have left you alone, abstained from your business because you are useful to us. We have done well for ourselves as you've executed your plans. But there were the same before you and there will be the same after you. And we endure."

The rider's pumpkin head roared to life, the flames stretching nearly a foot from the carved features of the face. "This boy seeks to steal an item of great power, a power I have gained much control of and that I will shortly use to bring the world of humans to its knees! This serves us all. But I must know what he knows and what he intends."

Martin looked anxiously from the riders to the devils and back again, feeling like a mouse between two cats. No sooner had this thought left his mind than Lilith came hurtling out of the cave, a long black feather clutched in her jaws.

"Go. Now!" she said through clenched teeth.

Martin held the lantern before him, it flared and a ripple formed in the near distance.

* * *

The shimmer that marked the opening in the veil was perhaps two dozen yards from where Martin stood. It was a straight shot. He had no choice but to run for it. The rider astride his great black mount could easily close the distance and beat him to it—or, worse, through it. His only advantage was the rider had jutting stones to navigate and Martin's path was relatively clear.

Lilith launched herself out of his arms and ran for it. Then Martin made his move.

The rider threw his pumpkin-head even as his horse reared and began to gallop. The jack-o'-lantern smashed against a pillar of stone, missing Martin by a few feet—flaming chunks of pumpkin raining down around him.

Lilith reached the shimmering curtain and turned to watch Martin's flight, her ears flat back against her skull.

Martin stumbled. The rider was going to beat him. The assembled demons howled and laughed, cackled and called. Martin recovered and pumped his legs as hard as he could. He shouted to Lilith, "Don't wait. Get the quill back!" But Lilith remained.

The horseman cleared the jagged maw of stones and had a straight path to where Lilith stood. Martin didn't know if the rider would be more interested in him or the veil. He didn't have his army with him, but perhaps getting across himself would be enough.

Refusing to quit, even with defeat clearly laid out before him, Martin pushed himself to his body's limits in a final sprint.

What could only be described as a battle-cry erupted from beyond the veil and, as the rider came within feet of it, his mount was struck broadside with incredible force. Antlers beneath its belly, Baxter heaved and toppled the steed, sending the rider sprawling. The reindeer stopped, lowered its neck to aim her antlers directly for the rider and grunted with menace.

Horseman and mount clambered to their feet. The rider reached for the reins of his horse, but the great, black stallion snorted and backed away. As it did, the rider's tack and saddle decayed, turned to dust and disappeared on the wind.

"Climb on, sugah!" Baxter said to a stunned Martin, who wasted no time following orders.

Chapter 36

Lilith was the first to come through. By the look in her eyes, Dale could tell they were running from something. A turkey feather was clutched in her mouth. Not a full second later, Baxter thundered through, Martin on her back with one arm wrapped around the reindeer's neck and a turnip on a rope held in the other hand.

The shimmering, flickering veil Dale had watched Baxter race into and now out of, faded from existence, but not before he spotted—briefly—a hulk of a man who appeared to have nothing above his shoulders running towards them.

"Martin! Are you hurt? Was that—"

Baxter caught her breath and answered for him, "The headless horseman."

Martin, having taken a moment to gather himself said, "I don't think after what you just did he's a horseman anymore, head or no head." He climbed off Baxter's back and set the turnip down at his feet. He crouched next to Lilith, and the feline dropped the quill into his hands.

"You got it? It was there? How—"

Martin stood and said, "Rumor was that the *former*-horseman was gathering objects of power, objects full of Jack-o'-Lightning. Scouts—it was ravens—the scouts were ravens. They learned what some of the objects were and tracked down the location of one of his . . . stashes." He held the object out before him and placed it in Dale's open palm.

It was magnificent. To anyone alive before the twentieth century, it probably looked like a humble turkey feather with a small metal nib, like those used to write any-old-thing. To Dale, it was an artist's brush, a sculptor's chisel.

"Martin," he said. "I don't know what to do with it. Is it enough just having it on this side?"

Martin shook his head and said, "I honestly don't know. I was hoping you'd find a use for it, or its rightful home. Please tell me you changed your mind. Please tell me you've written something."

At first, Dale's expression was stoic. He looked Martin directly in the eyes, took a long slow breath and said, "And it's coming along wonderfully." Then he cracked a wide, proud smile.

Neither of them expected the statement to result in a hug, but it did—briefly. Martin said, "What day is it? How long have I been gone? I need to get home."

Baxter answered. "It's been six days. Halloween is the day after tomorrow. I've visited your parents a couple times to check on them. They're worried sick. Charlie checked in on them, too. He had friends on the other side listening and keeping an eye out for you, so they know you're alive, but we'd better go."

The lantern flickered and Martin picked it up once more. Then, he looked down and Lilith, as though reading his thoughts, said, "I'll make my way back. Don't worry."

She glanced up at Dale and added, "Mr. Connors here might need a cat in his life."

Chapter 37

Much had happened in the days since Martin had crossed over. He wouldn't learn of it all until he'd had some time to recover, but a touch of it became clear when Baxter went in for a landing in front of his house.

Every window was lit with a purple-bulbed candle that flickered eerily and cast shadows through the skeins of spiders' webs hung from corner to corner. A dozen jack-o'-lanterns lined the front steps. There was the one he'd carved into the plastic pumpkin, but the rest were new. At first, Martin didn't want to go anywhere near a pumpkin with a flame inside, but appreciation won out over latent-terror. Among the carvings was one Martin recognized clearly as the face of Gump. This helped reduce his fear response, and he smiled.

A raven croaked three times and swooped down from whatever tree he'd been in and landed on the porch railing—right atop a bit of taped-in-place foam padding his father had probably secured for just that reason.

Mr. and Mrs. Kelly ran through the front door and down the stairs. Martin raced toward them and wrapped his arms around them. Tears streamed down Mom's face and she said things like, "We were so worried," "You had us so scared," and "We didn't know if you were coming back," between sobs. Mr. Kelly patted his son's back over and over and said nothing. He couldn't summon the words.

Martin let go of his parents and turned to survey the lawn, "I like what you've done with the place." In addition to the dressed windows and the jack-o'-lanterns, Martin's parents had created a cemetery in the front lawn, complete with fog and eerie-sounds machine. A dozen plastic bats hung upside down from the branch of one tree, and an enormous spider crawled up another. They had thought of everything.

Mom said, "We didn't know what else to do. We searched for you, but we knew where you'd gone. Your friends said . . . we were getting word you were alive and . . . we couldn't come after you. Trust me, your father spent three sleepless nights searching the strangest websites trying to find a way. Charlie told us what the rest of your . . . team were up to—just wait 'til you hear about that—so . . . "

"So, we . . . did what we could. I told the neighbors we were going to do it and how fun it would be if we really spooked the place up for trick-or-treat."

"Oh! Speaking of trick-or-treat," Mom said, "I've been thinking about your costume."

Martin hugged Baxter around the neck, thanked Charlie, and told them he'd be back out to see them in a little while—maybe after he'd gotten some sleep. Then, he followed his parents into the house so they could share stories.

* * *

Charlie had not been able to convince all the ravens he could find, but word did spread quickly among his kind on the humans' side of the veil. Those who spent most of their time in the mortal world did so, in part, because they had no love of the rider and what had become of the various worlds under his self-appointed rule. The ravens convinced one another to join the effort and it was only a matter of days before both US coasts and most of northern Europe had conspiracies willing to join the cause. And where there weren't ravens, there were murders of crows—cousins who filled the same roles as ravens in the mythologies of their native lands.

Thousands of black birds stood ready.

When the order came, or the suggestion since ravens don't take orders and are more than happy to tell you that, great clouds of birds filled the sky. They circled and swooped. They flew in strange geometric patterns. They swirled like twisters of beaks, claws, and jet-black feathers.

In the places where the great flapping clouds darted, smaller birds darted away and rodents ran for their lives. Black cats everywhere snarled.

News channels and YouTubers caught videos and shared them with their respective audiences. This attention exploded when the birds began gathering in staggering numbers in graveyards, around churches, outside schools and on playground equipment in parks. Though menacing, the birds were careful. They didn't cause property damage or intentionally startle babies and the elderly. They scattered when a hunter turned up with a rifle.

Birds flew by the dozens down busy streets, flapping close enough to pedestrians to riffle their hair or snatch food from their hands. Their croak and caws filled the air, and everywhere they went, the air crackled with Jack-o'-Lightning.

* * *

The black cats of the earth, found on nearly every continent, joined the scare three days after the birds. They didn't want to execute their plan at the same time and split people's attention. Rather, they wanted their role to continue the scare. Naturally, they wanted their own moment to shine as well.

The cats had almost all been happy to join in, if for no other reason than to outshine the ravens. They followed Lilith's suggestions to great effect. "Don't slink in the shadows; strut down sidewalks. Sit in front of people and stare at them. Howl in the night and make sure they could be seen by street lamp or porch light. Follow your people and stare into their eyes. Lurk in the shadows where you normally would not."

Where there were large numbers of them, they followed the same approach as the ravens, circling around graveyards, perching on every level surface and statue outside municipal buildings, and staring through the windows of schools. Naturally, they crossed every path they could.

It all made the news, blew up on social media. Instagram was flooded with eerie pictures of the gathered beasts of feather and claw. The lightning struck wherever the birds had gathered and crackled wherever the cats went out of their way to be unsettling.

The best part of their work wasn't the immediate scares, though. It was the residual curiosity they left behind. Legends about ravens, crows, and cats in a variety of cultures, all over the world were dredged up and made news or told around kitchen tables. The strangeness of it, the possible otherworldliness of it, was what sustained the increase in power.

* * *

There were too few goblins on earth to lend the kind of help the cats or ravens could be to one another. Even had they been more numerous, goblins didn't have the same kind of network. Goblins have a network of a different kind: Children, especially children with a penchant towards orneriness.

Gump's plan to recruit the adolescents of Carlisle had been highly effective, and—to his extreme delight—his recruits enticed their friends. Social media took care of the rest. After one enterprising youth took video of Gump looking his gobliny best, explaining what he needed, the hashtag #pranksforgump began trending across platforms.

Amidst the ravens, crows, and cats, jack-o'-lanterns began appearing on porches and in windows, on stairs, in the crooks of trees, atop grave-markers, and on rooftops. Gump could feel the familiar "something happening" and was delighted.

* * *

What none of them had counted on was that as lightning spread, there were creatures on the mortal side of the veil whose attention was called. Jack-o'-Lightning brought the spirits of this world to life. It woke long-dormant ghosts, and those ghosts, spirits, and poltergeists resumed hauntings they had abandoned years ago. Stories of hauntings spread quickly, though not as quickly as news of the hordes of cats and ravens. The spirits began to dance. People began to notice something frightening and exciting was happening in their world—it was happening more than any of them could remember. And no one could explain it.

* * *

One man *could* explain it. Dale had successfully reached almost all his contacts, who reached out to theirs, and together they had begun to flood their communities with scary short stories. They sponsored or otherwise encouraged contests in schools in their localities for the most terrifying shorts. The stories were gathered on a newly launched scare-site which quickly gained popularity, fueled by the growing interest in the spooky and otherworldly.

Renowned authors of the craft caught word and joined the fun. They started booking readings of their works in libraries and bookstores. Some released previously unreleased works. And this inspired movie houses to play films they hadn't played in years. Classic horror movie nights were scheduled and response was overwhelming. In many towns, tickets sold out for movies like *The Mummy*, *Fall of the House of Usher*, and *Poltergeist*.

There was no doubt there was a swell of power in the world that hadn't been there before. There were great thunderheads of Jack-o'-Lightning in pockets around the earth. If Martin's story was true, this meant there was less of the stuff on the other side of the veil, less power for the rider and his forces to draw from. Dale didn't know if it was enough, or if he'd have any way of knowing until the time came and the hordes of the undead appeared on the horizon . . . or they didn't.

Halloween was only a few days away. Then they would know for certain.

Chapter 38

Not everyone goes trick-or-treating with a goblin sidekick. Not everyone heads off into the night with a raven wishing them well from the front porch. Not everyone celebrates Halloween as a triumph over the forces of darkness invading the mortal world. Martin Kelly was unique.

Baxter had returned with his family and the pumpkin-carving elves to the north. She'd offered to update Sidney until Martin had a chance to catch up with her himself. Lilith was in Maine with Dale Connors. Gump turned up on the Kellys' front porch, imploring Martin to bring him along when he went, "Treat-treat-treat collecting."

Charlie had returned from what he referred to as a scouting mission with a report he thought Martin would be eager to hear. "He isn't the horseman anymore. Rumor has it, he's lost the mantle all together. He's grown another pumpkin head, they're saying, but this one spouts no fire. That great steed of his won't even let him mount."

Martin grinned and said, "So he's the headless walker now?"

"It appears that way. Far less intimidating, I'd say."

"And his power? The power on that side?"

"Hard to measure," Charlie said, "But the balance certainly appears to have shifted. The rider—walker—has lost credibility. He was bested by a mortal boy. No one will follow him now."

"We're safe?" Martin's mother asked.

Charlie said, "From this threat, certainly, and I'd wager it will be many years, perhaps generations, before another attempt is considered. Besides, I believe the balance is restored, if not tipped a little in this world's direction."

Mom and Dad let out twin deep breaths. .

They didn't want to let their son out of their sight after his prolonged absence, but they knew how important Halloween was to him and knew he only had another Halloween or two before he was too old to trick-or-treat. They stood at the top of the porch, watching Martin make the final adjustments to his costume.

"Don't be out long, Buster," Mom said.

"I won't," Martin said.

Dad said, "Be careful. I heard there are a lot of pranksters out tonight," and looked at Gump.

The goblin smiled and clapped his hands.

"Do you have glow sticks?" said Mom.

Martin reached into the pillowcase he carried for collecting candy and was halted when the turnip on one of the porch steps started flashing.

"Jack?" Martin said.

A thin wisp of smoke snaked from the lantern. It swirled and thickened. Martin knew what was happening and waited patiently. His parents said nothing either, having a strong suspicion they too knew what they were witnessing.

In less than half a minute, the semi-transparent form of Jack of the lantern stood at the bottom of the porch steps. He inclined his head towards Martin's parents. "Beggin' your pardon, Mr. and Mrs. Kelly, but I thought I might play a role in the lad's adventure tonight."

Mom and Dad both cocked their heads, and Mom said, "Haven't you . . . I mean, don't you think . . ."

Dad finished for her, "Don't you think you've had enough adventure together these last couple of weeks?"

Jack smiled and said, "Aye. I can see your point, but I feel rather sure we won't be chased by any demons or crossing any flaming rivers this night."

"Wait. What?" Mom said, head hands going to her face.

Martin said, "Nothing, Mom. It's fine. He turned to Jack and said, "You can follow along if you like."

"I had another idea, boyo." He gestured towards the lantern.

Martin's eyes widened. "But isn't keeping it real like that going to drain you?"

"A little, but I'd say there's enough of that lightning cracklin' around I shouldn't need to worry about it."

"Martin," Dad said. "What are you two talking about?"

Jack turned to Mr. Kelly and said, "I was suggesting rather than these green glowing sticks or a simple flashlight, your lad could use a lantern. It would look nice with the costume, I'd say, and add a little mystery too."

Martin's mom nodded and said, "Makes perfect sense to me. You'll keep the road well lit for him?"

"Would have it no other way."

Martin looked at the spirit in silence a moment and said, "Jack, after tonight—after Halloween—what are you going to do? Are you going back to the other side? Are you staying here?"

"There's nothing on the other side for me, lad. I'll have to return sooner or later, but there's enough power for me to tap into on this side for a while and I'd rather wait for as long as I can to see how things settle over there. Besides. . . I thought it might be nice to hang around a bit . . . get to know me family."

Dad shook his head, smiling. Mom said, "As long as you aren't bringing any more trouble with you, you're welcome here, Uncle Jack."

Jack's spirit seemed to glow. He bowed to Mrs. Kelly and turned to Mr. Kelly. Dad said, "I can't say we've ever invited a ghost for company, but you're welcome. No tricks. No trouble."

"No, sir. Thank you, sir."

Mom said, "There's a trunk in the attic that's been in the family for generations. It's full of family photos and journals. We'll bring it down while you two are out."

"I can't thank you enough."

Throughout their conversation, Gump and Charlie had been chatting quietly together. But it was clear from the goblin's dancing from one foot to the other and the increasing rate at which he was chomping his nails, he was getting antsy.

"We better get going," Martin said.

The smoky mist that was Jack coiled back into the turnip, and it glowed brightly. Gump pranced to Martin's side and they headed down the driveway together—a goblin dressed as an elf, and a fourteen-year-old-boy in a bright purple, inflatable headless horseman costume, carrying two pillowcases to stuff with candy, and a turnip occupied by Jack of the lantern.

Epilogue

Dale placed the quill gently on his desk. It belonged in a museum. For now, it played a role. He wasn't sure exactly what it was, but it couldn't play that role under glass. Martin had done his part. According to Lilith, a whole host of characters had played their parts, many of whom Dale hadn't had the opportunity to meet. He knew he'd helped, but also knew he could do more to maintain the restored balance of power.

Poe had been an inspiration when he was growing up. Dale's earliest stories had been written to emulate the late-author's style, though he was certain he'd never captured it. Poe was a literary legend, a treasure. If anyone channeled Jack-o'-Lightning, it was Poe. His last quill was right there, on Dale's desk, recovered from the other side of death itself.

Dale sat, took up the quill gingerly running his fingers along it, twirling it slowly between them. The nib was worn and stained with ink. What words had last come from it? What possibly unfinished tale had it been prepared to tell?

"Unfinished tale . . ." Dale thought, and opened his spiral notebook.

The words poured from him—his words—his story, but he was certain he could feel the lightning pulsing from the quill. It pulsed in Dale too. His fingers tingled with it. The hairs on his arms stood. He'd foresworn it for years, carving out only the smallest, secret slices of time for himself to take up the task. But tonight, Dale Connors was a writer.

About the Author

I am an elementary school teacher. I have been a paperboy, dishwasher, bookseller, barista, apple picker, customer service manager, rental company manager, flooring installation manager, salesman, retail merchandiser, grocery-warehouse picker, house painter, convenient store clerk, supplement seller, and more.

I have two brothers between whom I am the middle child.

I was born in upstate New York, spent my elementary school years in Pennsylvania, graduated high school in Massachusetts, met my wife while living in Florida, migrated to Tennessee, and have lived in Ohio since 2011.

My first book, "Peppermint Lightning," was published in 2014.

You can connect with me on:

🌐 https://peppermintlightning.press

🐦 http://twitter.com/pmintlightning

📘 http://faceboom.com/peppermintlightningpress

🔗 http://instagram.com/peppermintlightning

Subscribe to my newsletter:

✉️ https://bit.ly/3kV0FR8

Also by Phillip Davis

Pepperming Lightning

There is a force that powers the Christmas spirit, a magic that makes lights shine brighter, cookies taste sweeter, and keeps reindeer in the air. It is a power as old as Christmas itself, an unseen electric current of kindness, cheer, and good will. That force is called peppermint lightning. It is fading and in need of a champion.

Sidney, a nine year old school girl from Pleasant, Ohio, full of peppermint lightning herself, is called upon to help restore that magic to its former glory. She is recruited by a hopeful elf, an English gingerbread man, a matronly reindeer, and a proud snowman to bring the spirit of Christmas, the peppermint lightning, back to a community that has lost theirs. If she fails in her task, the spark of the holiday will fade and with it all the magic of Christmas. Will her determination, her random acts of Christmas kindness, and a little holiday mischief be enough to put the spark back in the season?

Justice for the Missing

People are disappearing from America's National Parks. Rick Minor is one of those people.

On the first night of a whirlwind tour of Utah's Mighty Five, with his closest friends Matthew Conrad, a university research assistant and Dianne Chambers, an environmental activist, Rick wandered away from camp and vanished without a trace.

Matt and Dianne must join the hunt, but the standard work of search and rescue teams will not be enough. The clues Matthew stumbles on appear to point to the impossible.

When a stranger emerges, issuing cryptic warnings and pointing in directions Matthew would never think to look, it becomes clear there are powerful forces at work. The investigation to find a missing friend will lead Matt and Dianne to face a much larger question. What is really happening on America's public lands?

www.ingramcontent.com/pod-product-compliance
Lightning Source LLC
Chambersburg PA
CBHW050931120626
46552CB00001B/152